ROAD KILL

PAUL LEGER

Published by Red Press, 2021
info@redpress.co.za
www.redpress.co.za

ISBN 978-1-990952-98-2

Editor: Claire Strombeck
Cover design: Caitlin Truman-Baker
Typesetting & layout: Matthew Covarr
Printed & bound by: Pinetown Printers

To my mother - for instilling the love of words

Day 1

1

Hidden by the shade of the gnarled pepper tree, the driver of the black Nissan Navarra tracked the prey's movements through his binoculars: the ritual tapping of the road sign, the stopping midstride to take a piss in the veld, the tucking in of the vest, the tying, the retying of laces.

Taking his cue at eight hundred metres – the yellow (and still wet) daub of paint on a telephone pole – the driver placed the binocs on the passenger seat and turned the ignition key. The Navarra crawled out from its den and rolled slowly onto the tar. His focus locked on the prey – still a distant smudge – the driver eased his foot onto the accelerator.

The runner's outline came into view – hogging the centre

line, sidestepping the potholes as he ran. The driver's jaw muscles tightened as he pressed his foot deeper into the floor – unleashing a menacing growl from under the hood. At two hundred metres, the runner's features were now clearly visible. Long sinew and bone, wearing a vest and peak cap and blue Polycotton shorts. His biltongy arms swinging loosely at his side, head lolling on his shoulders, his gait relaxed. The cap was pulled down, fending off the morning sun that still sat low on the horizon.

The runner was now moving away from the solid centre line, aware of the Navarra's approach, but his stride still loose and free. Glancing at the speedometer, the driver stuck to his lane. He wasn't about to blow this one; it had been too long in the coming. Under the cap, the runner's expression was changing – puzzlement had replaced endorphin-fuelled confidence.

Twenty metres. With a precision born out of repeat experience, the driver ground his foot into the pedal and pulled hard right on the steering wheel. Caught in no-man's land between the centre line of the R434 between Brits and Edendal, and the yawing veld of the North West, the runner's face registered a flash of primal terror, before flesh and bone merged with hardened bulbar steel travelling at precisely one hundred and forty-six kilos an hour.

2

Leaning over his *AA Map of Southern Africa*, Steve Aldridge traced a finger northbound along the N14. From time to time the finger paused on a point of cartographical interest. He rolled the names around his mouth. It was like sucking on a pack of boiled sweets – each came with a unique flavour: Soetkraal, Brakfontein, Lemoenhoek, Rosedene, Soutpan. A thought struck him. It was so true what they said – life was about the journey, not the destination.

Venturing into the unknown, guided by a mass of black dots linked by a spider web on a piece of paper – this was the stuff of goosebumps. And that's where he and Tarryn were wired so differently, because she just didn't get it. He related fully with guys like Columbus, Vasco da Gama, David Livingstone, the Voortrekkers. Like Bruce Springsteen sang, he was also born to be free.

Aldridge stretched over the bonnet and flicked a scab of bird turd from the white paintwork – it was a good thing he hadn't gone for the metallic.

Like explorers recent, past, and present, he was dressed for the job: Cape Union shirt tucked into Cape Union multi-pocket khaki shorts, anti-glare Polaroids, and Hi-Tec ATs (All-Terrains) – after Crocs, the best shoes in the world, in his humble opinion. He didn't care what anybody said.

Aldridge folded the map and returned it to its plastic sleeve. He checked his watch. It was still early. He took a slow sip from his Crème Soda and leant back against the Fortuner. Man, did it feel good or what to be on the road again. He closed his eyes, savouring the fresh early morning forecourt air, the warm North West sun on his face. This was why modern-day humans worked – for moments like this. The past year at work had been a killer, what with the Supa-Lube Bearings launch hitting them smack in the middle of the recession and all.

He held up the can and studied the small print. It didn't matter half the ingredients were Greek to him, because there was nothing like a well-timed Crème Soda. Best of all, there were another eleven where this one came from – Kruger treat. Again, he checked his watch: seven fifty-five. Good thing they'd hit the road early. As long as he lived, he would never get why women took so long to sort themselves out, when he could tick off the three Ss in ten minutes flat. Not that he was complaining, or anything. On a day like this, he was more than happy to chill while Tarryn did her thing in the Ladies.

"Mornings!"

Aldridge squinted into the sun. A fellow traveller. One of those sunburnt guys in Mad Dog shorts and slops and mozzie-bitten ankles clawed into scabs – a veteran camper.

"Mornings."

"Nice day for travelling, or what?"

"Most definitely. Couldn't ask for better."

"Where you chappies headed?"

"Kruger."

"Nice. Very nice. Which camp?"

"Satara," said Aldridge.

"Not messing around. I like. Which gate you attacking from?

"Orpen."

"Orpen? If I was you, I would hit it south from Skukuza side. Especially pulling that baby behind you."

"Isn't Orpen quicker?"

"In the old days, maybe, but this is the New South Africa, my friend. The roads have gone to kak and gone. 'Specially the one to Orpen."

"Thanks for the tip. I must look at my map again. Where you guys on your way to?"

"'Toti. Visiting the old lady's people. Got themselves a mansion right on the sea like you won't believe. Any closer and you need a lifejacket and whistle. Did you also kip last night at the Municipal?"

"No, we drove straight from Sasolburg this morning. What was it like?"

"Nice lake for the kids, but hardcore. Got chowed to death by mozzies as big as bats." As if reminded, he lifted a leg and gave his ankle a hefty scratch. "But for a hundred bucks a night, you see me complaining?" He took a lick at his soft-serve, aimed it at the Fortuner. "How's she run?"

"I've only had her for two months, but so far, brilliantly," said Aldridge, experiencing a fuzzy feeling in the chest.

"The new technology that's come out with this model is—"

"Four by four?"

"Umm, no. Just diff lock. But for the type of travelling we do, we don't really need—"

"And thirsty as all hell I bet. That's ours there, the red Hyundai under the shade cloth. Bought it off my brother-in-law for an effing bargain – excuse the French. Goes like a Boeing. ABS, aircon, CD shuttle, fifteen kays per litre – you name it."

"Is it still on motorplan?"

"No ways. Who needs a rip-off motorplan when you've got reliability?"

"It's actually not that much when you stop and—"

"Shit, here I'm jabbering like a woman and I haven't even introduced myself. John Phillips." Phillips extended a freckly hand.

"Steve Aldridge. Nice to meet you, John."

Phillips lifted his arm to the sky and suctioned the dripping ice cream from under the cone. "You must try one of these. Only sixteen bucks … with Flakey." He aimed the cone at the service court. "I see the missus is howling for my blood. Can't live with them, can't live without the bladdy things. Anyways, say howzit to the elis for me."

"For sure, I'll do that. You guys must have a safe trip."

Aldridge took a sip of Crème Soda and watched John Phillips cross the forecourt and stop in front of the Mens to give his ankle another claw, before disappearing inside.

That was another thing Steve Aldridge loved about travelling – you always met such interesting people.

3

"Fok!"

This had to be the tenth time the sign had blown over. Truter's day hadn't even started, but his gut was telling him it was going to be a seriously bad one. And nobody to take it out on; that useless pen-pusher Delport was never around when he needed him.

The morning breeze whipped the dust around Truter's state-issue riot boots. He glared into the cloudless sky. One of those hot-as-hell days he despised. Minimum thirty-five in the shade, according to his hangover-skewed estimate. Not that there was any shade to speak of, because all that stood between the sun and his balding head was a scrawny acacia. He would take Durban humidity any day.

A jackhammer pounded behind Truter's eyes. He must be getting old. That, or the Three Ships wasn't what it used be. Cock on block, the cheapskates were cutting the whisky with methanol. He wouldn't put it past them, because these corporations were all the same. They didn't care a rat's arse for their customers, as long as they made a fat profit. Who was it who had told him about a Chinese company replacing milk powder with baby powder? Must have been Delport and his Google.

With this new-found knowledge at hand, Truter's hangover now made perfect sense: the Chinese had bought out Three Ships and were cutting it to increase profits. Unbelievable. He didn't trust the chinks further than he could spit.

Truter farted into the morning sky. He pushed back on his hips, stretching his aching groin – he should have sued SAPS Rugby Union for making him play prop. How many times had he told the coach he was born to play lock? More than he could count, that's how many.

A new thought had hatched in his brain and was crawling its way towards the light – his ex-brother-in-law, Ross. He was the one diluting the Three Ships with rotgut to save himself a few bucks. Once a cheapskate, always a cheapskate. Now that he stopped to think about it, he'd never trusted the guy, even when he was still married to his witch of a sister. The mere thought of Sharon triggered the vein on the side of his head into violent spasm. There was something all high and mighty about Ross. Him and his fake concern during and after the divorce, acting like some marriage counsellor, but in the meantime getting his rocks off somebody else's problems. Who did he think he was coming over to his flat with a bottle of whisky? Invasion of privacy, that's what it was, asking all those personal questions, snooping about the place like he owned it, going for a piss one time too many – what was that all about, anyway?

What the stuff, thought Truter, he had more important

things to worry about right now than Ross the Toss. Like getting the roadblock up and ready before the holiday traffic hit. He looked around him. What was called for was a heavy rock to stabilise his sign against the wind.

It now occurred to him that Delport should be doing this, not him, a high-ranking policeman. Problem was, you couldn't rely on Delport to organise a lap dance at a Teazers. When it came to practical matters, the guy was worse than useless; if he couldn't change a tyre on a patrol vehicle, or something as simple as squeezing the truth from a suspect, how was he going to man a roadblock? All Delport and the new-breed cops were good for was office work, when what Truter needed was someone to cover his back under fire. His radio crackled into life.

"Come in, Sergeant Truter. Over."

Truter reached into the vehicle. "Sergeant Truter!" he barked into the handset. "Is that you, Delport?" He rolled his eyes skywards.

"Yes, sir. Over."

"Over what? Forget it! Flippin' hell, Delport, can't you see I'm busy? This is the real world out here, not some office tea party."

"Sorry, sir, I just called in to alert you to a possible missing person's in your environs …"

"Wat se environs? Speak English, Delport. A missing person's, who?

"A Miss Bianca Reynolds …"

Truter felt his pants stiffen. "You telling me a white

chick has gone missing?"

"No, sir. Bianca Reynolds is the partner of the missing person's. According to her statement, her boyfriend went for a jog at six hundred hours on the R434 and hasn't been seen since. She says he's normally back by seven hundred hours. Over."

Truter had heard it all before. "Let me tell you what's going on here, Delport. Your so-called missing person is dipping it in on the side. And this Bianca chick, I bet she has a face like a dog's ringster. Am I right, or am I right?" Truter shifted uncomfortably on his feet. Something was starting to stir below.

"She's actually quite pretty, sir. Long dark hair and nice skin … She's convinced something bad has happened. Over."

"And I'm convinced she's wasting our time, Delport. Over and out!"

The stirring below could no longer be ignored. He cursed himself for not sorting it out before coming on duty, but this was proof of what happened when you had to do everything yourself: you ended up rushing. You ended up forgetting to take care of the little things. Like taking a crap before clocking in for work.

Truter shielded his eyes against the North West glare and studied the horizon. The R434 was still clear – not a vehicle or human in sight. He had to act quickly, because one couldn't mess around with these things.

He scanned the immediate terrain for a suitable

site; right where he stood appeared as good as any. He loosened his belt, his holster and radio dangling heavily from side to side. A horse on the home run, his bowels anticipated impending relief. With not a moment to spare, he dropped his pants and squatted down and gave himself over to the hissing deluge, gasping with pleasure as the nagging burden dropped from his body. He shifted his weight onto his good knee and marvelled at the steaming result. Nature was incredible. The body's ability to produce such volume at such regularity was a miracle. There was nothing more underrated in life than the deep spiritual satisfaction of a good boskak. It ranked right up there among life's true pleasures.

Truter craned forwards for a better view of the road. His back felt like an ironing board. He should have given up rugby when that quack had told him to. His uniform creaked under the weight of his belly. Wiry black tufts sprouted from the gaps between the buttons. He sighed contentedly, savouring the moment. Special occasions like these were not to be rushed.

Truter's ruminations were called up short and sudden with the realisation that his allocated roll of patrol toilet paper was sitting above the office filing cabinet. Pushing down a surge of panic, he weighed up the options. There weren't many. He tugged at the spiky veld grass bordering the tar – a last resort. He calculated the distance between himself and the patrol van – at least twenty metres by his reckoning, and a messy affair getting there, with uncertain outcome, since the vehicle contained nothing of use besides KFC takeaway polystyrene and Sparletta cans. He patted his shirt pockets – a chewed Bic pen, his pack of Pall Mall 20s, two sachets of Grandpa headache powder. A second surge of panic, stronger this time, rippled through his body. He peered down the R434 – still clear. He lifted himself into a half-squat, careful not to mess, gingerly probing his trousers for good news. Nothing in the front pockets. He was fast running out of options. Wincing, he reached round to his back pocket and patted the square outline of a charge book. He had forgotten about that. Things were looking up. A wave of Zen-like calm settled over him and the world felt like a kinder place.

Taking his time now to complete unfinished business, he paged through the dog-eared charge book, noting the contents with grim satisfaction. Pretoria couldn't accuse him of laziness. Not that those bastards ever showed any appreciation for his contribution towards law and order. They couldn't even spell A-P-R-E-S-I-A-T-I-O-N. It was a pity to see all his work about to go to waste. To think he had risked his life bringing some of these criminals to book. On the other hand, a charge book was nothing more than admin PT to make the bosses rich; his present situation was a lot more urgent than any donation to their gravy train.

His view crystal-clear on the matter, Truter took hold of carbon copies B500 to B535, ripped them from the charge book, and proceeded to wipe himself blue in the arse.

4

The midnight-blue Toyota Camry turned right into Rubicon, then swung a sharp left into Nerina Close. The driver cut the engine and coasted the car to a halt. Thirteen was the last house on the street.

Freddie Ferreira remained behind the wheel, surveying the lie of the land. Standard government-sponsored face-brick house built in the '70s, fronted by stoep and cement strip driveway. Neat flowerbed with white and yellow flowers of some sort, and an Italian statue – lady's touch. White Ford Sapphire parked under the shade cloth. Mint condition. Two thousand and four to 2006 model – Sunday driver.

Ferreira shifted his focus to the roof and gutters – as his mentor Mr Zeta would have said, the window into a man's soul. No peeling fascias, gutters and IBR in prime nick, no rust spots from what he could tell. Processing the data, Ferreira had his profile: not your average New South Africa citizens. These people lived to a financial plan. They lived for the future, not the present. He could just about smell the fear coming off the roof.

Ferreira flipped down the visor and checked his hair. Licked his finger and straightened his eyebrows. Gave his nostrils the all clear. He clicked open the gold-buckled vinyl briefcase on the seat next to him, checked the forms were in the correct order, and snapped the lid shut. The butterflies were kicking in. Same ones as in Angola, before a contact. Just different time and place.

"Nice and slow does it, boytjie. Nice and slow."

Ferreira stepped from the car and strode up to the gate, pushed it open and marched up to the front door and knocked.

He counted to ten. Footsteps were now coming his way. A shadow appeared behind the brown glass, followed by a chain unbolting. A crack of light escaped through the door, revealing a balding grey-haired man fronting a heavy gut.

"Yes?"

"Good mornings, Mr Scimper!" Ferreira announced. "Fred Ferreira, Titanium Financial Services. Hope I'm not too early?" The crack widened. Ferreira slipped his hand through, which Scimper ignored. Ferreira laughed. "Hell, hope I've got the right day? We did say Wednesday, nine o'clock?" The ball was back in the enemy's court. The man on the other side hesitated.

"I suppose you want to come in?"

"Thanks so much, sir. Beautiful day, don't you think?" Ferreira squeezed through the doorway.

"We'll do this in the lounge."

Scimper led the way down the passage. A bloodhound testing the air, Ferreira noted the trapped odours – burnt chip oil, bacon, Glade air deodoriser (lavender), old dog, ladies perfume. He followed Scimper into the sitting room. A woman was on the couch, knitting something brown.

"My wife, Joan. What did you say your name was again?"

"Ferreira, sir, Fred Ferreira. Pleasure to meet you, Mrs Scimper." Flashing a gold-toothed smile, he walked over to the couch and politely shook the woman's hand. "Lovely place you people have here. So … how can I say? … Tasteful." He noted the red flush to the cheeks, the lift of the heavy tits. He pointed at the brown something. "I see you're very creative. Something for your grandchild?"

"Take a seat," cut in Scimper. "I don't have much time."

Don't have much time se voet – only a bored white man on government pension would wash his car during the week.

"Yes, of course, sir, I understand fully."

Ferreira sat down and fiddled nervously with his tie. Scimper remained standing. *Oldest trick in the book – top dog, bottom dog.*

"Where did you say you were from again?"

"TFS. Titanium Financial Services, sir. I'm just here—"

"Ja, ja, you're just here to try sell us something, right?'

"Not at all. It's what we in the business call a courtesy visit."

"Give me a break."

Joan Scimper lifted herself from the couch. "Who would like a nice cup of coffee? You must be thirsty after driving all the way from …"

"Witbank. And a coffee would be fantastic."

"How much sugar?"

"Just three, thanks."

Brian Scimper waited until his wife had left the room. He pulled up the chair opposite Ferreira, and leant forwards. *Classic combat mode.* "Okay, pal, don't give me this nonsense about courtesy visit, blah blah. Before you start with your spiel, let's get a few things straight, man to man."

"Sure, Mr Scimper."

"First of all, you mustn't think I was born yesterday. I know what you insurance people are all about. You're like vultures. No, no, let me finish. I'm not saying you're one of them, but while you're under my roof, in my house, don't try pull a fast one over me." The shock on Ferreira's face didn't pass unnoticed. Scimper softened his assault. "I've seen every trick in the book, Ferreira. Been there, done that, got the T-shirt." Scimper blew into his hanky, and examined the result. "Okay, I've had my say. The stage is all yours, pal."

"Sir, I appreciate you being honest and all, but can I just say something? I ... we at Titanium would never sell you something you don't need. You have my word on that."

Scimper settled back into a more comfortable position – *aggro township brak exposing its soft underbelly*, as the boys liked to describe it. "Okay, that's good to hear. I'm glad we have an understanding. Now—"

"The other thing I want to say is I personally understand how hard retired people like you and the wife have worked for your money. I've been there, Mr Scimper, with my own mom and dad." Ferreira paused. "I don't want to get all personal, but my dad lost everything after this new government came into power. Forty years of pension savings down the drain because of the same vultures you mention. You won't believe it, but this was the reason I first got into the life insurance business."

Brian Scimper's face now carried the guilty look of a man who knew he had crossed the line. "Look, I didn't say you're one of them ..." he mumbled. "Anyways, here comes the coffee."

Ferreira held up his hands. "No need to explain. I understand hundred per cent where you are coming from. Mrs Scimper, don't tell me you baked those yourself? I don't know where you guys find the time." Helping himself to a crunchie, Ferreira turned back to the man. "But you're totally right, there are a lot of crooks out there. You can't drop your guard for a second. Not for one second!" He bit into the crunchie. Margarine, not butter. "Delicious. I could tell you some stories that will make your hair stand on end, but I don't want to waste your time."

"Ag, forget it, man, you've come all this bladdy way, so we might as well do things proper."

Ferreira stirred his coffee. He took a slow sip, leaving the client to stew. The man was an open book, with guilt written across his cancerous forehead: guilt for insulting him, guilt for reading him wrong.

"Is there something you want to show me?"

"Sorry, I almost forgot," laughed Ferreira. He placed his coffee carefully down on the doily and reached for his briefcase, then laid out the brochures and application form. "This is a lovely coffee table." He stroked the smooth Imbuia grain. "It must be valuable."

"Probably worth a few rands," said Brian Scimper, hooking a thumb in his wife's direction. "Belonged to her old man."

"Like my own dad used to say, you can't put value on sentimental things. Don't you agree, Mrs Scimper? It's like measuring love in rands and cents."

"Very true. We must remember that one, Brian."

"Anyways, to start with, Brian ... Sorry, you don't mind me calling you by your first name?"

"Ja, no, it's fine."

"Fantastic. I think you will find this page quite fascinating, what with your mathematical brain and all ... Statistics!" whispered Ferreira, injecting magical status into the word. Scimper leant forwards for a closer look; his gut cantilevered over the carpet. "I shouldn't do this, but I'm going to tell you guys a little secret. Everything in the life insurance business is run by statistics. You see these three charts, Brian? These tell us when people will die – whites, blacks, coloureds, Indians, you name it." Ferreira winked across to the couch. "And you thought only God could do that? I'm just joking, Mrs Scimper. The big brains at head office are constantly punching in information like someone's race, weight, height, job, where they live, what they eat, if they smoke, things like that. And once all this is punched in, the computer does the rest."

"Incredible."

Ferreira tapped the graph. "Take this one, for example. It tells you ninety per cent of retired white males in Gauteng will die before they turn sixty-eight years old!" Ferreira sat back and observed the impact of this rather worrying statistic. According to the file, the guy had just turned sixty-seven. The hook was now so firmly lodged he could allow some play. "I know you won't believe it, Mrs Scimper, but there are white people in this country who haven't planned for their family's financial future. It's terrible to see what's going on, especially in the cities. Boy, I could tell you some tragic stories, but I don't want to contaminate this lovely home with sadness and negativism."

Judging by their expectant faces, Ferreira could tell Brian and Joan Scimper didn't have an issue with their house being contaminated by sadness and negativism.

"You sure? What about ... you know?"

"She's fine."

"There are so many, I hardly know where to start ... Okay ... So, about a year ago this lady and her three beautiful young kids came into our office to sign some papers for the estate. Seriously tragic stuff, what with the husband dying in a head-on with a taxi on his way home from work ... so he could be at his daughter's birthday.

But the problem was, we couldn't help the lady because her husband had stopped paying his premiums two months before." Ferreira glanced across at the couch. "Tell me when to stop, Mrs Scimper … Okay, so now a couple of months later the estate is wrapped up, there are debts all over the place, the wife and kids have lost the house, the car – the whole shebang. You maybe want to block your ears, Mrs Scimper, because that's not the end of it."

Ferreira sucked in deeply. "Not much later I'm visiting an old client in Roodepoort, and at the robots I check this dirty-looking beggar with her cardboard sign and scruffy kids. Same old New South Africa story, so of course I don't think much of it. But now wait for it, Brian. Only after I get home and turn on the TV that it hits me like a dum-dum bullet straight between the eyes!"

"What does?" said Brian Scimper. His eyes were glowing.

"The woman and kids with the cardboard sign. One and the same who were in our office a few months before!"

"Oh, liewe Here," exclaimed Mrs Scimper, holding her hand over her mouth.

At this point, Ferreira stopped, cleared his throat, and continued in a soft whisper. "As long as I live, Mrs Scimper, I'll never get that picture out my brain." He cleared his throat again. "People have no idea how important it is to have comprehensive life cover."

Brian and Joan Scimper sat in stunned silence, contemplating the ghastly horrors of an unplanned future. Ferreira peered over his cup. The man looked drained, a beaten dog. Ferreira had caught him with a left hook. He had him up against the ropes, reeling, with no idea of the financial blood bath happening out in the streets.

"Mrs Scimper, I'm not here to tell your husband what to do. Like I said, this is a courtesy visit. All I can offer is my professional experience in such matters and advise in accordance. But after what I've seen, which is not pretty, I have four words of advice to my clients. DDTL. Don't ... Delay ... Too ... Long! The consequences are too tragic to think about."

With this, Freddie Ferreira nudged the TFS Life application form in Brian Scimper's direction.

5

Truter was finally a man at peace with the world. He stood back and admired his work. Supported by the patrol van's wheel jack, the Police Roadblock sign stood erect and paraat. The orange road cones lined up beautifully. His fold-up chair, lunch tin, pocket Bible, and thermos flask waited patiently under the acacia. Man, nature, and the R434 were at one.

This was where Truter felt closest to his maker. A subject he had in fact recently broached with Delport – the spiritual side of police work. It was like talking to a brick wall, because the guy was clueless when it came to things of a philosophical nature. Same went for the rest of the New South Africa police force.

The earlier gusts had dropped to a light breeze, and the air felt cooler. Clouds were gathering in the distant sky. Further down the tar, a crow was up to its neck in roadkill. Above him, the mossies were chirping in the branches. His police radio crackled in the background. It was altogether pleasant.

Truter coughed up a ball of phlegm, swirled it around his mouth, and launched it into space. He sighed. It was quite magical how his God worked. He ambled over to the acacia and reached into his lunch box.

He chewed slowly, savouring the egg-onion-polony combo. He contemplated the brown landscape, the dust dancing on the breeze, the minibus taxi approaching from twelve o'clock, the black smoke trailing in its wake. The vehicle lolled from side to side, meaning two of two things: fucked shocks and overloaded. Truter settled deeper into the fold-up. The tin coffin hurtled past, chased by a Venter trailer. According to his calcs, it was clocking hundred and forty – not bad for a ninety-something HiAce.

He watched the taxi disappear into the shimmering horizon. There were a million more where it came from, and he had seen enough Jap concertinas in the police yard to know that Nature had its own way of dealing with the problem. Truter reached into the ice-cream box for another egg-onion-polony. He could live off the bladdy things.

His reverie was interrupted by a crackle emerging from the far distance. For a brief moment, he was back in Angola, waking to a Caprivi dawn, the ta-ta-ta of an AK-47 floating across the Cunene. He levered himself from the foldup and stumbled across to the van.

"Now what, Delport?"

"Just checking all okay your side, sir? Over."

"Of course all is okay, man. Why wouldn't all be okay?"

"Over."

"Over what?"

"I was waiting for you to say *Over*, sir. You didn't say it. Over."

The earlier jackhammering in Truter's brain had returned with a vengeance.

"Jesus, Delport! Are you messing with my head, or what? Over and fucking out!"

Truter slammed the handset back into its holder and wiped the spittle from his chin. What was it about this guy? *All okay your side, sir?* Didn't the moegoe have anything better to do with his day? Like fighting crime, for instance. Who did Delport think he was – some headcase in need of a shrink? This was Pretoria all over. Personnel asking him how he was feeling, suggesting he talk to someone about the so-called "Incident" – in inverted commas. Meantime, back at the ranch, they were the ones with the problem, not him.

Even his GP, a so-called educated man, telling him to spend more time in nature. It would be good for his blood pressure and heartburn; it would bring down his cholesterol, blah, blah. He had seen the fax to Sharon's lawyer. *Unresolved post-traumatic stress disorder with physical complications.* Big words that meant squat.

Truter returned to the foldup and sat down heavily. He had lost his appetite. Constable Delport probably meant well in his own simple way. For a brief moment, a very brief moment, Truter considered getting back on the radio. He smiled grimly. What a prize doos ... Old Delport checking up that his superior was okay. There was a first for everything; this would never have happened in Angola, never mind Benoni Dog Unit.

Feeling calmer, Truter adjusted his Bondiblus and tilted forwards for a better view of the road. A white vehicle towing a caravan was approaching due south – holidaymaker by the looks of it. Holding onto the acacia, Truter pulled himself up. He hitched up his pants and patted his beloved .38. It was time to get back to work.

6

Business at 13 Nerina was moving at a nice pace. A very nice pace, indeed.

"That's it, you've got it, Brian! From your side, only four hundred and eighty rand a month. No strings attached, no small print. Plus, you get all those extra living benefits and rewards." Ferreira pulled out the photocopy from his flip file. "Joan, you will also find this interesting." The woman on the couch had long since abandoned her knitting. "Get a load of this. Pens, airtime, stainless-steel pots and pans, free holidays, you name it – that's what you get when you join our loyalty programme." He handed the brochure across the coffee table. "In fact, just the other day I bumped into one of our Elite Club members who had come back from a week's holiday at Lost City. Was apparently out of this world."

"Are you taking all of this in, Brian?"

"Let me get something straight, Freddie. Are we talking comprehensive here?"

"The full Monty, sir."

Scimper tugged at his ear. "I have to admit, I'm impressed."

"And did I mention that free funeral cover is included in the price?"

"You serious?"

"A hundred and ten per cent serious. Peace of mind means everything to us." Ferreira swivelled in the chair. "Ah, I see you've got your eye on those pots and pans, Joan. Nice, hey?" Ferreira swivelled back the other way. "If you don't mind me saying, Brian, you're looking a bit confused there. You want me to go through it again?"

"Ja, if you don't mind."

Ferreira registered the red glow around Scimper's ears. "No worries. You have to be an Einstein to understand the complicated formulas. Even I don't understand them. But basically, Brian, how it works is that Titanium subsidises your monthly premium. Every rand you put in, we, as your investment partner, put in another rand or two. So even the guy who could never afford boutique life insurance before, now suddenly can. It's what we call a win-win. You get your comprehensive, and we get a happy client."

The cat was out the bag. Ferreira watched Scimper chase after it.

"It's all quite fascinating, but …"

"But?"

"I mean, what's really in it for you guys?"

Ferreira's phone was vibrating in his pocket. "Sorry, Brian, you mind if I grab this one? An old client of mine."

Ferreira walked through to the dining room, over to the window – he registered the backyard with Portapool. "This better be important, china, I'm in the middle of a sell … Are you pulling my chain? … I don't believe what I'm hearing, Dippies. You swear you aren't bullshitting? … Okay, I believe you, but have you told him yet? … Well, you better do it pronto, china, or he's gonna strip his moer big time." Ferreira glanced back across the room. "Listen, I have to go. We'll connect later for a Blackie somewhere."

Ferreira walked back into the living room. Sat down. Grinned. Focussed.

"Sorry about that. What was I saying now? Oh, ja … Brian, our mission at Titanium is to remove the obstacles standing between you and genuine comprehensive life cover. Like I tell all my clients, whites in the New South Africa also deserve peace of mind, not just the ANC fat cats and their buddies. I'm sure you agree?"

"Hundred per cent, Freddie. This government is out to destroy the white man. After all we did for them." Scimper's wife nodded in the background.

"And that is why we must stand together – ons moet saam staan – and come up with tailormade solutions that fit your needs. You can just initial there and there, Brian. Don't worry about all that stuff on the back; it's just a formality to keep the lawyers happy."

"You sure?" said Scimper, his hand hesitating above the page. Ferreira chuckled.

"Trust me, Brian, nobody ever reads this page, not even us. It's basically mumbo jumbo talk for Titanium being the other beneficiary because of the subsidy thing, and the terms and conditions for the loyalty prizes. Nothing to worry about there, Joan, you'll be getting your pots and pans in no time."

"It all sounds so fantastic."

"It is fantastic." Ferreira reached across and gently prised the form from Scimper's hand. "Brian, as long as you've initialled and signed the last page, I say we're A for Away!"

7

Sergeant Clinton Truter, SAPS Edendal, North West Province, stepped boldly into the road and flagged down the approaching Toyota Fortuner. Forced to take sudden evasive action, the caravan snaked back and forth like a wounded puffadder, eventually straightened, and came to a shuddering halt in a cloud of gravel and dust fifty metres down the road.

Truter smiled in grim satisfaction, confident he had established an early psychological edge. The prey was aware of the hunter's presence, but still unsure of his intentions – a good sign. Truter shifted into stalk mode, a tried-and-tested SAPS tactic when approaching skittish criminals. Moving slowly, he brought his body in line with the driver's rear-view mirror, folded his arms, and rocked back and forth on his heels – "marinating" was the technical term for it. There was still no sign of life from the Fortuner, bettering the odds for a clean kill. Experience had taught Truter things could get messy if the prey made a sudden attempt to climb out the vehicle.

One hand resting on the butt of his revolver, Truter approached the caravan. Raw animal instinct had now taken over where Homo sapiens left off. He was a lion stalking a wounded wildebeest separated from its herd. He was Clint Eastwood in *Dirty Larry*. He was Arnold whatsisname in *Total Recall*. His cyborg brain was crunching through the data. "FS" registration – hadn't his ex shacked up with a dumb poes from the Free State after the divorce? Maybe Fortuner boy and him were related. Truter studied the back of the caravan – a Jurgens 401 – nice one, pal. White Fortuner 2.4 GLS. A moffie four by two. Bought second-hand or new? Both ways, it must have cost a packet – meaning, Fortuner boy had cash to blow. Personally, he wouldn't have gone for white.

Processing these pertinent facts, Truter had his profile. This was going to be easier than shaking a meercat from a tree.

He could now see himself in the extended side mirrors. He admired his bulging thighs. His forearms looked pumped as all hell. The Bondiblus had been a good buy. He shifted his mind to the task at hand. Besides attempted murder, there wasn't much to pin on Fortuner boy; he had his bases well covered. New tyres all round, not a scratch in sight, no point even checking the licences. Hell, there was even a double reflector strip running down the side of the caravan. Not that any of this deterred Truter, because he considered himself a man of great imagination.

Sidling up to the driver's window, he took a step back and locked into *Engage* – legs apart, knees slightly bent, right hand resting loosely on gun. You couldn't take any chances in these troubled times.

Still fairly confident this was another of those routine Arrive Alive campaigns the minister rolled out every year in the interests of holiday road safety, Steve Aldridge rolled down the window. Visible policing, they called it. He had no problem with that; it meant the police were doing their job. In his mind, taxpayer money well spent and a small price to pay for the minor inconvenience.

"Morning, officer," Aldridge said, attempting the delicate balance between white-on-white familiarity and respect for an officer of the law.

There was neither response nor movement from the tower of vacuum-packed meat behind the sunglasses. Uneasiness replaced quiet confidence.

"Ask him what's wrong," whispered Tarryn.

Aldridge cleared the lump from his throat. "Is there a problem, officer?"

"Sir, please step out from the vehicle," growled the police officer. It was the dangerous low growl of a pit bull.

Startled by the menacing tone, Aldridge remained stuck to his seat.

"I will repeat, sir. Remove yourself from the said vehicle."

"Steven, you better do as he says."

"Ja, no, of course," said Aldridge, fumbling with the belt buckle. "They must be checking for unlicensed weapons and aren't taking any chances." This rationale for the officer's threatening tone lent a measure of reassurance to the situation. After all, the South African Police Services were there to serve and protect law-abiding people like him and Tarryn.

Aldridge climbed out the Fortuner and came face to shoulder with the police officer. Removed from the safety of his vehicle, it was now all too apparent what he was dealing with: a dangerous animal. He didn't have a good feeling about this. Not a good feeling at all.

"Sir, turn around and face the vehicle. Thank you. Now place your hands up on the roof and open your legs."

Aldridge wasn't sure he had heard right. "Excuse me?"

"Now! Wider, sir!" Barely able to support his own weight, Aldridge spread his jellied legs. A rough hand explored the inside of his thighs and calves, his stomach and his chest. "No concealed weapons, sir?" The voice contained disappointment. "You can turn around."

Aldridge turned. His head was reeling. "I'm not a criminal, if that's—"

"Not a criminal? You call driving like a psycho not a criminal?"

"What? I can't believe this—"

The police officer raised an open paw to the sky. The effect was instant and powerful. For a second the world returned to absolute silence. Almost tranquil.

"Sir, luister carefully." A finger thicker than a Russian sausage pressed into Aldridge's chest. "Don't you have respect for the law of this country?" Prod. "Don't you know there is innocent women and children walking the streets?" Prod. "Don't you—" Tarryn, rising from the passenger side of the Fortuner, had diverted the officer's attention. "Lady, please remain seated in the vehicle!" he bellowed.

"Okay, okay, but at least you can tell us what's going on? We've done nothing wrong."

"Step back into the vehicle, lady!" the officer ordered. "You don't want this husband of yours to be in more trouble than he already is. He is your husband?" he asked, as if hoping to add immoral offences to the growing list.

"I can't believe this … Of course he's my husband!"

"Please, just do what he says, Tarryn. It's all a big misunderstanding."

"You be a good wife and do like your husband says. You feeling more relaxed now, Meneer?" enquired the officer in an altogether more pleasant tone. He reached into his pocket and retrieved a Bic and the remains of a charge book. "There is one thing I have learnt, and that is people never learn." He flipped through the pages. "No matter how hard we try to show you people right from wrong, you never listen. Must I tell you why? It's because people have lost respect for each other in this New South Africa. It's not like the old days. Nowadays everyone's in it for themselves. There's no gemeenskap. How do you call it in English? … Ja, community spirit. There's no community spirit." The police officer sucked on his pen, formulating his thoughts. "You think my job is easy, sir? You think I like standing here in the sun, risking my life, facing down hardened criminals day after day? These modern ones think nothing of pulling a gun and shooting you in the face. They have fokol respect for life.

You understand what I'm saying?" Too dazed to reply, Aldridge nodded weakly. "Don't move, Meneer." The policeman walked to the front of the Fortuner and noted down the licence plate details. "Us white men have to work together. Ons moet saamwerk." He ambled back to Aldridge. "Don't look so worried, I'm not here to make kak for you. I can see you are going on a holiday, you with your caravan and your nice wifey in there. So this one time I will be easy on you. I will forget you attempted grievous bodily harm to a police officer. What you say about that?"

"Thank you," whispered Aldridge. "I really appreciate it."

"No problem." The officer hesitated, as if reconsidering this act of supreme generosity. Then, without further hesitation, he tore the page from his charge book, crushed it into a ball, and tucked it into Aldridge's Old Khaki pocket. "There you go, sir. You and your wife must drive safe now, because there's crazy people out there."

8

"What a flipping bastard!"

"You shouldn't swear like that."

Aldridge glanced nervously into the side mirror. So far still nothing. He was rattled. Seriously rattled. It was just a matter of time before the white police van gave chase.

Like in that movie, *Hitchhiker* – except, this was for real.

"I don't care. He is a bastard. Who does he think he is, treating us like common criminals? I don't know how you could just stand there and take his abuse."

"What did you expect me to do, Tarryn? You could see for yourself the guy meant business. Jeepers, he had his hand on his gun the whole time. You didn't see that, did you now?" As if Aldridge didn't have enough on his plate without his own wife turning against him. She had no idea what he was dealing with back there; he'd spent enough holidays in Kruger to recognise the eyes of a predator.

"Why us? Why not someone who deserves it?"

"I don't know … These guys must face danger every day. He probably thought we were acting suspicious or something …"

Aldridge trailed off. None of it made sense, no matter how he looked at it. The South African Police Services were there to serve and protect. That's what they were paid to do. That's why he paid his taxes. A black cop treating a white man badly he could maybe understand, but a white cop treating a white guy this way? He must have had his reasons.

"Listen to yourself trying to defend him! He picked on us because we were a soft target. Finish and klaar."

Last time Aldridge had seen Tarryn worked up like this was when that idiot had driven into them outside the mall in Vanderbijlpark and claimed it was their fault.

"Maybe we should try calm down?"

"And maybe the police should go after the real criminals? Like that taxi and trailer overtaking us on the white line. That's who they should be pulling over, not us."

Aldridge stole another glance into the side mirror – he was tempting Fate, but he couldn't help it. By now the cop would have radioed his buddies up ahead. This was what came of taking leave before year-end. Tarryn's hand pressed into his thigh, giving it her trademark rub-and-squeeze.

"You're right, babes, let's just forget it. Why should we let some sadist spoil our holiday? What you say?"

"I agree." Aldridge dropped the visor. Women were much better at handling these things; they saw the world differently, more from a distance. "You notice how the landscape's changing? It's already getting more hilly and pretty." Sure, Africa had its problems – poverty, overpopulation, Aids, crime, Ebola, the Corona virus, wars everywhere and all that – but it was still an amazing continent. At least South Africa didn't have ISIS. "Won't you pass me my sunglasses cloth from the cubbyhole? This sun is hitting me straight in the eyes."

"Sure. You want me to clean them for you?"

"That'll be good."

Fourteen minutes had passed and still no flashing blue light or roadblock. By now he would have caught up with them.

"Here you go. Nice and clean."

"Thanks … What?"

"You look like that cop on TV."

"Who?"

"I'm trying to think. Flip, it's on the tip of my tongue."

"You mean *CHIPS?* John Baker and Eric Estrada. I used to love that programme—"

"Excuse me, I'm not that old. No, not *CHIPS* … Don Johnson! That's who you look like."

"You really think so?"

"Would I say it if I didn't mean it? Remember how we used to watch it at your mom and dad's place, before we got our own TV. What was it called again?"

"*Miami Vice.*"

"Of course! This stress is causing me to lose my memory." Tarryn flipped down her visor and pouted. "What you think of my new lipstick? It's called 'Summer Rouge'."

"I like it."

"Me too. Talking of memory, did you hear about Pierre's mom being diagnosed with Alzheimer's and all? Sandra told me."

"You serious? That's terrible."

"Worse than terrible – it's tragic. It sounds like she'll end up moving in with them. That, or they have to put her in a home. If I was them, I would go for that option."

"I would feel bad putting my mom in a home."

"You say that now, babes, but imagine the kids seeing their gran like that. It's not fair on them. Not to mention dangerous."

"Why dangerous? Geez, this sun's seriously bad. I can hardly see."

"Well, if you stop and think about it, it's scary what could happen. For instance, imagine Pierre and Sandy are out having supper somewhere, like they need to spend quality time together. Pierre's mom in the meanwhile decides she's hungry and switches on the stove. Next thing, because of the Alzheimer's she forgets about it and the house catches on fire. Just the thought gives me the grils. Especially with those Trellidors all over the— Shit, what was that loud bang!"

Gripping hard onto the steering wheel, Aldridge pumped the brakes. "We must have hit something!"

"Sounds like it's scraping on the tar, Steve. You better stop. There's an open place just up ahead there."

Aldridge eased the Fortuner off the road and brought it to an uneasy standstill. He stared wide-eyed at the road ahead. He felt the blood draining fast from his face.

"This isn't good. This isn't good at all."

"You better go see what's wrong, Stevie."

Aldridge unclicked his seatbelt and climbed out. His back suddenly felt stiff and sore, his body a lead weight. He walked slowly towards the front of the Fortuner, bracing for the worst. He looked down. Lifted his arms in despair. Below him, the Fortuner's fender dangled like the leg of a landmine victim. Oily water was pooling fast around the shattered mess – a steaming stain on the parched earth. Tarryn's shadow appeared alongside.

"Oh, shit!

"I can't believe it. I just can't believe it."

"Now, what do we do?"

Aldridge rolled his head from side to side, trying to stave off a storm cloud of despair. He squatted down, took hold of the mangled fender, lifted it to one side. He peered underneath.

"We must have hit something big. The radiator's totally buckled."

"What, like an animal?"

"Must have been a buck. Tarryn, the water's pouring out."

"I can't believe this is happening, babes. Shit, shit, shit!"

First the cop. Now this. It was a nightmare coming true. Aldridge pulled himself to his feet. His head felt woozy. He stared into the threatening African void. This was what came of taking leave.

"We're in the middle of nowhere."

"We'll make a plan, Steve. Do you think we can make it to the next town?"

Aldridge took a deep breath. "Only if we can stop the leak."

"How far do we have to go?"

"Must be at least twenty kays. I'll have to check on the map."

"What about the spoiler?"

"Fender."

"Spoiler, fender, whatever. Can you fix it?"

"I'm not sure. I can try tie it with some line from the Fold-Away." Aldridge sucked in air, then dropped to his hands and knees for a calmer assessment. "I can actually see the hole … I could try plug it … We have that five-litre water in the back … It might just get us to the next town."

"You really think so?"

Aldridge sat up, dusting himself off. "I don't know, but maybe I can make a plan with this." He suddenly felt up for the challenge. He would show Tarryn what he could do. "But we better get something to catch the last bit of water."

"I've got that empty feta tub we can use?"

"That'll work."

"And how about a Crème Soda while I'm at it?"

"Now you're talking my language."

"You've got some grass in your hair … Here, let me help you."

"Is it out?"

"Ja. You know what else?"

"What?"

"I'm glad I chose you instead of Russel Stevens."

"Me too."

Aldridge walked over to the caravan, determined not to let this latest get him down. After all, wasn't it the definition of adventure? Expecting the unexpected, facing a challenge head-on? Like the American guy said at the company bosberaad: the only thing standing between you and achieving the impossible is attitude. *Spelt with a capital A, gentlemen*. With the right Attitude, one could achieve anything. South Africans knew it more than any nation on earth. There was a reason for the saying, 'n boer maak—

A dusty running shoe in front of the caravan door had caught his eye. One of those Nikey numbers stacked on the stands outside Pep. Was it only in South Africa one came across lonely shoes in the middle of nowhere? Someone could write a book on the subject; it would sell like hotcakes. He stepped in for a closer look. Strange. It was the real deal – a Nike Pegasus. Besides the dust, it looked practically new. No ways it could have fallen off a bakkie carrying farm labourers. Aldridge dropped down and peered under the Jurgens – no harm checking. A moment later he stumbled backwards.

"Babe, what's wrong? Has something stung you?"

Unable to mouth coherent speech, Aldridge pointed at the underside of the caravan.

Balancing the Crème Sodas on the ground, Tarryn walked over to where he was pointing, and bent down for a first-hand look. "What, is it the—"

She blinked. Then blinked again. It couldn't be. But it was. A human being. A human being wrapped around the tow bar. Gazing up at her with a bewildered expression. Dressed in a vest and jogging shorts. The foot nearest to her was wearing a Nike running shoe. The other foot was wearing a black sock with a hole in the big toe. The man was dead. Deader than a dodo.

9

"Steven, just think straight for one minute. We can't leave him here. Imagine what it's going to look like … First you get stopped for speeding. A few minutes later you drive over someone. They'll say it's a hit and run. You … *We* won't have a leg to stand on. They'll throw away the key. They'll … Oh my God, what are we going to do?" Tarryn Aldridge sucked in deep for air. Bit down hard on her lip.

Her husband of twelve and a half years could barely manage a whisper. "I wasn't speeding. You saw how the sun was in my eyes. I didn't see him. I swear on the Bible I didn't see him."

Tarryn gazed into the morning vista of brown koppies. Her moment of panic had come and gone; she now felt strangely calm – like watching a movie of herself from high above. Curled up against the tree, Steve reminded her of an abandoned orphan creature from Animal Planet. It was an odd sensation seeing him like that.

Someone had to take control. She walked over to the tree. Her tone was now slow and measured. "Look me in the eyes, babes. Think how this is going to look in a court of law. It'll make no difference if you were speeding or not, because it's their word against ours. Who do you think the judge will believe? Us or that cop?" Taking her husband by the shoulders, she shook him gently. "Are you listening to me? We have to decide what we're going to do, and we have to decide now."

"This is all a nightmare. Please tell me this is a nightmare." The long slow moan that followed was more animal than human. And it scared her.

Softly-softly clearly wasn't working – he was too far gone. Tarryn couldn't afford to be dragged down with him. She released his grip on her leg and pushed him away.

"What will they give you for hit and run? Twenty years? Thirty? Life? Think about it – you'll be an old man before they let you out of jail. But hey, you're right, let's sit here and wait for Officer Psycho. I bet he's packing up this very minute and coming back for lunch at the Wimpy." Her words were stinging and barbed and more effective than a swarm of angry bees.

Aldridge jolted upright, his eyes staring and wild. A trail of crystallised spit ran down his chin. "What do you want us to do?"

"That's better." Tarryn's mind was working fast; she had already played out the options. There weren't many. "We *have* to move him. If we don't, they'll trace him back to us. They have our details and our tracks are all over the place. We might as well leave a note for them. You understand what I am saying?"

Aldridge nodded weakly. "Like move him where?"

"I'm thinking … We can't dump him in the veld; they'll find him in no time. We have to find someplace else, far away as possible from here, so they can't make the connection."

A wave of fresh horror washed over Aldridge's face. "You mean he has to come with us in the car?"

"Unless you want to call a taxi. Why, have you got any other bright-spark ideas?"

"But—"

"Thought so. He can flippin' go in the caravan if it will make you feel better—" Tarryn brought a finger to her lips. "What's that noise?"

"What? What can you hear?"

"Shit, I think a car's coming."

The words were barely out her mouth when a white vehicle – a white police van, to be precise – floated into view. Bearing down on them, its engine whining under the strain, time and space hung suspended. The van hurtled past. Steve and Tarryn Aldridge stared at each other in wide-eyed terror. Even at speed, there was no mistaking the driver.

"We've got to get out of here, babes!"

This time around her husband required little encouragement. In fact, he appeared positively revived by the latest brush with the law. He stepped past Tarryn and pulled open the caravan door. "Let's do it!"

"Where you going?"

"To fetch the groundsheet."

Swallowing hard, Tarryn Aldridge approached the twisted heap wrapped around the tow bar. It seemed so small and frail. More jogging short and vest than flesh and bone.

"I don't know how you can look," croaked Aldridge.

Tarryn reached down and tentatively took hold of a skinny ankle. The skin was cold – sort of Checkers-fresh-chicken cold. She pulled on the ankle. It pulled back. She pulled harder. It wouldn't budge.

"You need to help me here. He's stuck."

"What must I do?"

"Grab the other leg."

Aldridge crouched down beside her. Trying not to look, he groped underneath the caravan for the other ankle – the one with the shoe.

"You ready?"

"I think I'm going to be sick."

"Not now, Steve. Okay, on the count of three. One … two … three!"

"He's not moving."

"Let's try again. But pull harder this time. One, two, three, pull!"

Tarryn gave it all she had. At first, nothing happened. But then, the sound of tearing polyester and a dull thud as the body dropped to the ground.

"Let's get him into the veld, behind the tree."

Clutching an ankle apiece, they dragged the corpse across the open, and into the grass.

"You can let go now, Steve."

The man lay spread-eagled on his back, his face gazing into the cloudless sky. His right arm lay loosely at his side, his left twisted and broken behind his back. The shorts were blue polycotton. The Zeerust Half-Marathon vest was shredded. He was covered in brown dust. There wasn't much blood, but this didn't make him any less awful. His lip was curled back. His front teeth were smashed to smithereens. Tarryn stared down at him, transfixed by the odd little details. She couldn't make out if he was white or coloured – come to think of it, she wasn't even sure they had coloureds in this part of the country. His eyes were misty green. He looked about Steve's age – forty, forty-five-ish. He looked confused. Which was understandable.

"The groundsheet, Steve."

Aldridge unwrapped the blue groundsheet and spread it open next to the body.

"I can't believe this is happening—"

"Please, sweetie, this isn't the time. I'll take the top, you do the legs, and we'll roll him onto it. You ready?"

"No, but let's do it."

They flipped the body over, facedown.

"Again."

The body now lay on the edge of the groundsheet, face up. Taking hold of the corners, they proceeded to roll the sheet with the body. For some odd reason it reminded Tarryn of the time she made chicken wraps for Steve's mom and dad.

"We're almost there! You lead the way." They lifted the blue vinyl shroud and walked it slowly to the caravan. "Okay, one, two, lift." Aldridge heaved the head of the bundle into the caravan, climbed in, and dragged it across the linoleum. "All the way to the back … Okay, that's fine … You better cover him with the duvet."

Keeping guard at the caravan window, Tarryn stretched her back; this was more of a workout than Curves. She watched her husband drape the new Mr Price duvet over the blue package. It was like watching a clumsy robot at work.

"Enough faffing, Steve. It's fine."

"You sure?"

"Yes, I'm sure. Please, can we just get the heck out of here!"

10

Hot and cranky, Truter headed back to the station. The half-pack of Grandpas he'd tossed back over the course of the morning had long since thrown in the towel; his hangover had returned in great swathes of sweeping cranial pain. It was now all too obvious he should have stayed in bed and called in sick, and gifted Delport the favour of experiencing the burden of responsibility first-hand.

The morning had been a total write-off. After Fortuner boy, zilch, not a stitch of action. Nothing but taxi after taxi heading up to Limpopo. If he'd known things were going to be deader than Boksburg State Mortuary, he wouldn't have let Fortuner boy off so lightly. What was he thinking? On reflection, he wouldn't have said no to that wife of his. Blonde chicks did it for him; it didn't matter the blonde came straight out a bottle. If he could rewind the tape and start over, he would play it differently next time. He wouldn't even bother with Fortuner boy. He would start on the passenger side, invite her out of the car, do a full body check for concealed weapons. He would take it nice and slow, no rough stuff; she would love it and be begging for more of the same. Why decent-looking women went for slapgatte like Fortuner boy was beyond understanding. It could only be the money and fancy caravan holidays. Gold diggers, the lot of them. Sharon all over again. Divorce was the best thing that had ever happened to him. Good riddance to bad rubbish was all he had to say on the subject.

The raw memory of Sharon had Truter scratching in the cubbyhole for his Grandpas. The box came up empty. He crushed it in his fist, screwed down the window and tossed it to the wind.

The van screamed into the station yard and came to a skidding halt next to Delport's white Corsa. Truter waited for the dust cloud to pass, before lifting himself out, slamming the door and lumbering up the concrete steps.

"Fokken hot or what out there!" He slapped the counter. "What's up, Poortjie?"

Constable Delport winced. He lifted his head from behind the mountain of brown case folders.

"Afternoon, Sergeant. Sorry, I mean, morning."

"Good morning, good afternoon, good evening. Hell, Delport, what's making you so deurmekaar there?"

"Just sorting through some dockets, sir."

Adrian Delport was a bony bird of a man, cursed with red hair, glasses, and a pale complexion – a combination ill-suited both to Africa and the South African Police Services. Truter had formally drawn attention to this plain fact in his letter to Pretoria, requesting Delport's transfer back to where he had come from – Ladysmith or some other lady-boy sounding place. As the letter explained, it was clear as day his deputy's appearance undermined public morale. Following the chain of logic, this in turn undermined his own morale, which in turn undermined the morale of the South African Police Services. Which wasn't a good thing, since morale was already at an all-time low. Three months on, Truter was still awaiting a reply, which proved that Pretoria didn't care a pimply arse about what was happening on the ground. Next time, he wouldn't bother.

Although Truter had written off Delport as a crime-fighting machine, even an idiot could see what the man lacked in physical presence he made up in administrative diligence. In fact, Truter had slowly come to realise Delport's physical deficiencies suited him just fine, because the only thing he hated more than money-grabbing cockteasers, Pretoria fat cats, and meddling ex-brothers-in-law, was petty admin. Truter had zero tolerance for it. Admin was an insult to his intelligence and his true calling. God had put him on this earth to serve his country, to get his hands dirty, to fight crime on the streets head-on. God did not put him on earth to fill in multi-coloured forms. His unspoken arrangement with Delport therefore suited him just fine. He got to fight crime and Pretoria got their forms.

Truter walked casually around the counter and flicked the back of Delport's head. "So, what's so interesting in those folders?

Delport adjusted his glasses. "Just the usual stuff, sir."

"Just the usual stuff, what? Who's been getting up to kak in my absence?"

Delport had distilled the open dockets into a one-page summary. Bracing for the inevitable, he started at the top.

"One. Attempted break-in at 24 Florence Road. The next- door neighbour says she allegedly saw the Witbooi brothers loitering there early this morning—"

"Allegedly my foot. Of course it's them." Truter made a mental note. Little donders. Even if they denied it, he would sort out the Witbooi twins good and proper. This was one policing principle he shared with Delport: prevention was better than cure. "Next?"

"Two. Report of drunk and disorderly behaviour outside Manie's Off-sales. Mr Floris wants us to charge the culprits, but he doesn't want them to know it's him. I said he will have to—"

Truter sunk his fist into the counter, causing Delport to drop his pen. "I swear, next time I see that dronkie Hans

Gariep and his kakke hanging around the pavement asking for money and matches, I'm going to snap their skinny necks and let them cook in the van for a day. That will teach them about the dangers of drunk and disorderly." Truter's migraine was fast subsiding in anticipation of the physical pleasures that lay ahead. "What else is on that paper of yours?"

"Just some township stuff." Delport rattled quickly through the list, aware his boss didn't have time for what went on in the township. "Shebeen stabbing, theft of a Mazda 323, shack fire, two reports of assault with intent to do grievous bodily harm—"

"Okay, okay, Delport, I get the picture," said Truter, disappointed there was nothing juicier on the table. "Is that it?"

There was of course the growing mountain of open dockets that Delport would have to mention at some point, but this wasn't the time to bring up the war. "There's the missing person's—"

"Ja, ja, I know about that one. Or have you already forgotten?"

"No, sir. It's just that the wife phoned again twice to say he didn't take his diabetes medication before he left, and now she's seriously worried he will—"

"Delport, do you see two of me standing here? No, you don't. I will get to it, when I get to it, you understand?"

"Yes, sir." Delport held up a fax. "This came in from Pretoria. I think there's meant to be two pages, but we've run out of fax paper."

Truter reached over the desk and snatched the fax out his hand.

"What the hell do they want this time? *To all station commanders …*" He read through the contents, mouthing the words. "Stuff them, Delport. If they want this information, they must get off their lui arses and come dig it up for themselves. I bet you half these stats are already sitting in their files."

"It looks like the Department needs more detail on the mortuary stats. It could have to do with an investigation that's going on," Delport ventured tentatively. "Or maybe they just want to feed it into the national database."

"I don't care if they want to feed it into their ringsters, Delport. We don't have time or manpower to do their dirty work for them. Don't they know I have a missing person's case and all this other stuff to attend to? If Pretoria wants my stats, they must come here and ask me personally. Bugger that!"

Considering the matter closed, Truter rolled the fax into a ball and dropped it on Delport's desk. According to the SAPS handbook, this amounted to subordination, but Truter knew that Delport wasn't about to voice an opinion. The man was ardently respectful of rank. Truter also respected rank – as long as it was below him. Anything higher, he didn't care a toss about.

11

Jakkals Venter swirled the single malt back and forth, savouring more the idea than the taste of burnt Briketts. He swallowed. Shuddered. Red Heart and Coke won hands down, but it was the thought that counted. How many daughters would cough up five hundred bucks for a bottle of whisky for their old man? Zero.

Jakkals contemplated his middle-ageing legs – the hair was something else. Same went for the knotty tangle of varicose veins. He yawned. Days didn't get more perfect than this. Any other man would consider himself blessed, spending his birthday at home with family and all.

"How's the whisky, Pa?" Melanie shouted from the pool. "Jissus, not so tight, Ryan. You're choking me!"

What was it about that little shit? Forever hanging on to Melanie, like some orphan monkey clinging to a game ranger. Enough to drive one nuts. He didn't buy Melanie's "just a growth phase" talk. Psycho speak for "fokken irritating". Not that he was going to start telling his daughter how to raise her kids, but in the old days a solid slap would have sorted Ryan out one time.

"Smooth as velvet, sweetie." To prove it, Jakkals lifted the glass and downed the dregs. His molars crunched into an ice block. Five hundred bucks was a rip-off for the stuff. "Thanks again, hey."

Jakkals reached into his shirt and tugged distractedly at

the curly black tuft sprouting from his navel. He was in one of those heavy birthday moods that seemed to get worse with each passing year. Fifty-four was neither here nor there. In no time he would be staring sixty hard in its ugly face. Jesus, he could still remember the day his dad turned sixty. It felt like yesterday. And where was he now? Pushing up daisies in the Roodepoort state cemetery. Life's a bitch and then you die – whoever psycho came up with that one had a point.

The landline was ringing. They could call him on his cell. Across the pool, Christina lifted the towel from her face.

"You not going to get it?"

"No."

"Maybe it's important. Please answer, Jakkie."

"Ja, okay, keep your hair on." This wasn't the woman he'd married thirty years ago. She had become this panicky bird banging up against the window – the smallest thing sent her off the deep end. Rolling his body off the Addis lounger, he caught sight of his reflection in the glass sliding doors – not the prettiest sight in a Speedo, but at least he was still alive. Same couldn't be said for half his buddies.

Venter's home office faced directly on to the pool and braai lapa. He pulled open the sliding door. The phone was still ringing. Covered wall-to-wall above his desk were his hunting trophies – a pissed-off warthog with heavy eyebrows holding centre-stage. Below them, his photos.

Chrissie and him at their place on the Vaal. Next to it, a misty studio photo of the family looking ridiculous in their Sunday best – her idea, not his. One of him holding up the hammerhead he'd caught off Stilbaai beach on New Year's Eve. And his favourite – a yellowing blown-up photo of him and the boys partying under an Angola sunset, shirts off, downing Blackie quarts around the fire, eating meat straight off the spit. All of them pissed as coots, with him holding court in the middle. He was still built like a brick in those days; not an ounce of fat.

"Jakkals Venter … Jissus, Dippies, why the hell don't you call my cell? … Well then, the battery must be flat, but still. What's up? You're sounding jumpier than a fucken grasshopper … Sorry, boet, hold on a sec." Jakkals held his hand over the mouthpiece. Melanie was standing at the door, drying the snivelling kid. Fuck, if it wasn't one thing … "Sweets, I'm just on an important call here—"

"Sorry, Pa, I didn't mean … Mom said I could get a plaster from you … Ryan's cut himself."

"Ask Betty inside. She knows where they are." As if he needed this crap on his birthday. "Okay, speak to me, Dippies." He shoved his hand into his Speedo and gave the underside of his ballbag a gouging claw. He'd kept meaning to top up with Mycota; the itch was getting worse by the day. "Whoa, hold your horses. What you mean, disappeared? … Let me understand this correct, step by step. You did the usual, exactly to the T. But because you heard nothing on the channels, you decided to circle back later. Right? … How much later, Dippies? Fifteen minutes, one hour, two hours? … Let's settle on forty-five minutes. At this point you discover there's nothing there. Risen up like fucking Lazarus … Seriously, I don't need to hear this. You sure you double-checked the hospitals and morgues? … I'm just asking. And no, I'm not saying you didn't do a professional job … Whoa, Dippies, no need to get your ball bag in a knot … Listen up. I want you and Freddie to keep looking until I say stop. You get me? … Good, because we can't afford mistakes this stage of the game, 'specially mistakes costing me big bucks … And one more thing, Dippies. Next time you call me on my cell, not my bladdy landline."

Jakkals slammed down the phone. Dipshit! This was what he got for listening to Chrissie. He should have stayed put in the lounger. Any minute now this thing would start chewing at his ulcer. There had to be a logical explanation for it. There always was, as long as you were prepared to look for it. Jakkals sniffed his fingers. Winced. The rash was definitely getting worse. He would have to Google "Athlete's Foot of the scrotum" when he got back to the office.

12

"I told you already, Tarryn, I can't go any faster! The engine will blow if we don't pull over soon."

"Are you crazy? We can't stop here."

"Why not?"

"It's not safe. There must be a quiet farm road nearby." Tarryn leant across the seat. The needle still had another bit to go before it hit the top of the red. "Please, just keep driving for a bit longer? There has to be somewhere … How far did you say the next town was?"

"How am I supposed to know? Five kays. Maybe less. Maybe more."

Like an ageing Windows computer, Aldridge's panic-riddled brain was at that precise moment attempting a hard drive reboot to clear it of all recent cached memory, the contents of which included: a psycho cop with fingers thicker than pork sausages and the body odour of a dangerous animal; a dead body with skinny legs and a grinning mouth of smashed teeth; a mangled fender scraping the tar like chalk across a blackboard; a blistered big toe with a curved nail poking through a black sock; drying blood on a blue groundsheet.

"There it is!"

Aldridge snapped back to the present. To the front of them, an oval sign loomed large and threatening:

WELKOM TO EDENDAL
WHERE STRANGERS LEAVE AS FRIENDS

A wounded soldier returning from the front line, the stricken Fortuner limped past the sign, trailing a thin line of water.

Edendal wasn't your average North West town. It was beyond average. More arid, more desolate, more rundown than anything the Aldridges had hitherto passed through on their way to Kruger. It was new millennium South Africa at its best.

Turning left into Hoof, the Fortuner entered what was presumably once the commercial centre – treeless, potholed, lined by barricaded shops. A Kwaito track blasted from a Star Furnishers. Next to it, a Happy Cash Loans and a butchery fronted by rolls of lumo-pink sausage and sheep heads grinning at the passersby. Sprawled on the pavement, a red-eyed huddle bounced a Castle quart. The Fortuner kept moving. Tarryn and Steve Aldridge kept their eyes locked to the front.

"You would swear this place has never seen tourists before."

The knot in Aldridge's gut ratcheted up a notch, and with it came a fresh wave of nausea. Coming to the four-way stop, a dog of indeterminate bloodline blocked their path. Tarryn stretched over and pressed on the hooter.

"Jeepers, don't do that!" said Aldridge, alarmed. "People will look at us."

"What – do you want us to sit here all day instead?"

The cur stood up, lifted its leg against the front wheel, and dragged itself onto the kerb.

"This place gives me the grils," said Tarryn. "There's no white people anywhere."

"Tell me about it."

"What do you want to do?"

"I dunno. What do you want to do?"

Invisible eyes were watching their every move – Aldridge felt them all over his skin. The human brain was wired to smell death, so it was just a matter of time before someone tipped off the cops. The Focus-on-the-Positive he'd learnt on the Dale Carnegie course wasn't working, for the simple reason there was nothing positive to focus on. But one thing he was sure of: his life was over. He had killed a man. He, Steven John Aldridge, had killed another human being. He already saw the headline splashed across the lampposts: "Sasolburg Man in Hit and Run Murder". He saw his friends, the guys at the office, his dad opening the *Sasol Herald* and seeing the headline and photo from his ID book. That Deborah Patter woman from eTV would flock to Sasolburg to interview the neighbours. Everybody and their dog would have an opinion. How they couldn't believe a quiet guy like him could murder somebody. But then it just went to show you couldn't judge a book by its cover. Saying how lucky they were, because it could have been one of them. Or worse, one of their kids.

The warning buzzer was screaming for attention. The needle was up against the plastic pin. Steam was rising from the bonnet.

"Please Tarryn, we have to stop – the engine's about to

explode!"

"All right, we'll stop then. Let's find a caravan park where we can stay the night."

"But what about *him*?"

Tarryn considered this for a moment. "We'll put him in the boot."

"There's no ways I'm sleeping with him in the boot. Seriously, I can't take this anymore—"

"Okay, okay, in that case we'll find a B&B. Happy now?"

"But what if someone finds him?"

"Who's going to find him? Jesus, it's only for one night; we'll be long gone before anyone wakes up. And you're talking like we actually have a choice in the matter. You yourself said the engine is about to explode. So, until we get it fixed, we can't go anywhere. Right or wrong?"

Clenching her jaw against the fear and what-ifs breeding like flies, Tarryn softened her tone.

"Come, drive just a little more. There has to be somewhere to stay close by."

"What's that in front there?"

She had also spotted the sign. "I told you so … Eden Palm. I like the sound of that."

"Come on, you can do it," whispered Aldridge into the dash. "Just a little bit more."

"Turn left here … into Nerina Close"

The Fortuner shuddered and steamed and jerked along Nerina – a gravel street hiving off into cracked cement driveways and 1970-something face-brick houses with thirsty yards, netting curtains and front doors fortified by Trelli.

"Only fifty metres to go," said Tarryn.

"Let's just pray they have space for us."

"I'm sure they do." She squeezed his arm. "Left again." The Fortuner turned into Rubicon. The buzzer had now kicked into high gear. The light flashed red and angry. "Just a few more seconds, Stevie, we're so close now." She bit into her lip.

Tarryn's brain was racing ahead of itself; she had it all mapped out. They would settle in, unpack, run a nice hot bubble bath, prepare a tasty snack. She could heat up the doggy bag of ribs and chips from the Wagon Wheel and make a tomato and onion salad to go with it. They would eat and relax, and only then plan their next move. She was going to get them out of this, no matter what it took.

"That must be it there."

"You think so?"

Aldridge switched off the engine. Crackling sounds, accompanied by a cloud of steam floated up from under the bonnet. They stared silently at the yellow-on-green sign wired to the gatepost:

Eden Palm B&B.
Where strangers become friends.
Wir Sprechen de Deutsche.
No cheques! No credit cards!

Vibracrete ran the length of the property; above it, a mesh of razor wire. The driveway was all tar. The garden was devoid of green. The windows were few and small.

"It doesn't exactly look friendly," said Tarryn.

"Maybe we should try find something else?"

The Fortuner answered with an anguished groan of contracting metal.

"I suppose we better find out if they have a room for us. You want to ask, or must I?"

"Maybe we should both go?"

They climbed out and approached the gate. A chain with a Viro padlock blocked the way.

"Looks like there's nobody here," said Aldridge, hopefully.

"You better try the bell … Dumb place to put it."

Aldridge extended his arm through the gate, his cheek pressing up hard against the bars. He pressed the button. Unseen to his left, a brown blur was bulleting across the tarmac. Aldridge leapt back in fright as it flung itself against the gate in a frenzy of saliva and snarling teeth.

"It almost took my bloody hand off! I don't need this in my life. I seriously don't."

The rabid animal continued its onslaught against the gate.

"Adolf! Platz!" boomed a voice.

Deaf, or feigning deafness, Adolf resumed his assault with renewed gusto – as if aware time was not on his side. A stocky individual in khaki shorts and Crocs with white socks was making his way down the driveway.

"Adolfus! I said, platz!"

The man walked casually up to the gate, grabbed Adolf by the collar, yanked him onto his hind legs, and gave the leather a sharp twist, switching off the oxygen tap. With instant effect.

"That's my boy," purred the man. He relaxed his grip and stroked the dog's whimpering head. He turned his attention to the couple, standing far back from the gate. "Sorry for this," he said. "Adolf sometimes gets a little excited with strangers." The man knelt down. Adolf licked his face. "You're such a big baby, ja? You just don't like to be teased, isn't that so?" The man stood up, looked Tarryn up and down, and turned to her husband. "So, what can I do you good people for?"

13

Ferdie Meyer slid the combo clipper-nail file back into its vinyl sheath, sat back and admired the result. In this business, a man's hands defined one; they were the difference between success and failure. Like, who would buy a classy package from a director with grease monkey hands? He reached to his side, yanked on the lever, and tilted the chair back to P/2.

"I'm telling you, Trutes," he said, stroking the suede

finish. "They don't make quality like this any more. Nowadays it's all plastic Chinese crap. Guess what I paid for it?"

"How much?"

"Guess."

"I give up."

"Come on, take a guess."

"Fok, okay … Seven hundred bucks?"

"Five-O! Fifty. Can you bladdy believe it? Scored it at a liquidation auction in Boksburg. Same with half the stuff here."

Meyer's office was a simple and functional affair in keeping with the economic status and general tastes of his clients. Arranged on a diamond-patterned carpet from the Joshua Doore in Nigel were his swivel Executive Chair, a beech-veneer desk and a pair of white plastic chairs of the posher garden variety. Set at an angle on his desk was a misty picture of him and Amanda and the kids in an ornate gold frame. Next to the photo, an AVBOB-sponsored calendar and a box of tissues.

"How's your drink doing?"

"Still lekker, Ferdie … Ag, what the hell, you can gooi me a top-up."

"That's my man." Meyer reached over and emptied the dregs into Sergeant Truter's glass. He flicked a nail clipping onto the carpet. "Lemme see that pic again, in case he comes in."

Truter handed Meyer the photo of a younger Gary

Johnson with his shirt off, holding up a fish. "Nice size barbie. Did you try the body shop in Brits? He might be lying on ice there."

"Why would they cart him all the way there?"

"Because you never know with these State-employed monkeys. What about the hospital?"

"Checked. Like I told my pen-pushing deputy, the boytjie's absconded and giving some chick the hot meat injection as we speak."

"You're right. Nobody evaporates into thin air. Not in this place.

Truter threw back the last slug and stared morosely into the bottom of the glass. "Good stuff this."

"The best. Way better value than that rip-off Johnnie Walker Red. You see what they're selling it for now? Over two hundred bucks!" Meyer spotted another errant nail clipping wedged under the family photo. What Amanda saw in that dress was beyond him – it made her tits look all droopy before their time. He licked his finger and retrieved the nail. He took a nibble. "Anyways, what were we talking about again?"

"About playing your cards right."

"Oh, ja. Take me, for example. I bought this business just after the elections. Everyone thought I was cooked. Even my own toppies. Said I would be bankrupt in a year. Like, what black man will use a white man's business when he can go to a fly-by-night in the location for half the price?" Meyer snapped his fingers. "But I showed them,

Trutes. I checked the writing on the wall and I adapted myself to fit. It was the same in the car game. You can't keep selling HiAces when the government is forcing taxi owners to buy the new Quantum. You change your tune. You get your act together and you start selling Quantums."

"Hey, I've got a good one for you, Ferdie … What does HiAce stand for?"

"Dunno."

"High Impact African Culling Equipment!" Truter slapped the desk. "Fok, I love it. High Impact African Culling Equipment."

"Ja, it's a good one. But that's exactly what I did. I adapted my business model to fit the market. And look where I'm now. Sitting comfy. You check that pile of folders up there? Ninety per cent of them blacks – my bread and butter. If I had to wait around for my white clients to peg off, I would be out of business yonks ago. The things live forever nowadays."

"I see what you saying."

"And you check that Insurance Claims box next to it? That, pal, is where the big money is today."

"How so?"

Meyer crossed his legs on the desk. "John Smith signs up for a fat funeral plan. John Smith pegs off. John Smith's family claims on the funeral plan. Insurance company pays me direct – velvet-lined casket, full embalming, black Merc, fancy snacks afterwards, you name it, all the whistles and bells. And no questions asked. Ka-ching! Money's in the bank, and I'm happy as Larry."

"Nice."

"Nice for me, double nice for the small-time insurance brokers making themselves a fat packet on commission from the big boys – the Santams and Liberty Lifes. These guppies are coining it all the way to the bank." Meyer flipped open the brown folder on his desk. "For instance, check this one for old Roger Henley. Signed up for the full Monty on 12 May – I'm talking this year. Five months later he kicks it and scores the Lotto with an all-expenses-paid funeral. How's that for a luck?" Meyer pushed the policy across the desk.

"Who the hell is Roger Henley?"

"Roger Henley, man. You know him. The big rooikop who came second in the darts round robin last month?"

"Oh, him. I didn't know he pegged."

Meyer clicked his fingers. "Just like that. Keeled over in the street walking back from the club on Tuesday night. I didn't realise he was such a big mother. My boys took serious strain lifting him into the van."

"How did he peg?"

"Asthma attack, according to the DS. I'd show him to you if I had the time, but blue in the face like you've never seen. Looked like he had choked to death." Meyer followed the policeman's gaze. He lifted the whisky bottle. "Sorry, man, we've klapped it dood. You want Lynette to make you a Nescafe?"

"No, I'm good. Anyways, I must hit the road." Truter

flicked the policy back in Meyer's direction.

"Same here. We're gaaning on like there's no tomorrow." There was a knock on the door. His secretary, Lynette. Wearing that short red number again; the one that drove Meyer nuts. If she wasn't a reborn and married to his cousin, he would do her some serious damage. Pretending to act not interested – who did she think she was kidding?

"Sorry to disturb, Ferdie, but Mrs Henley's here."

"Okay, give me a sec to get organised. She can fill in the claim form so long."

Meyer and Truter followed Lynette's arse out the door. Meyer sighed. "Enough to give you serious sack ache." He pulled on the lever; snapping the Exec to upright. For months now he'd been meaning to sort out the mechanism, but with things so busy he hardly had time to piss any more. "Back to the grindstone, Trutes, but I'll keep you posted if the Johnson boy comes in."

Meyer saw Truter out and shut the door. The guy reminded him of a psycho Rottweiler – all cute and cuddly until the thing ripped your head off. He lifted his jacket off the hook. A black sports number, a little frayed at the elbows and collar and a small tear dating back to a recent funeral where the sharp edge of a coffin had hooked. These minor defects aside, the jacket befitted a man of Meyer's professional status. He returned to his desk and prepped the scene. Family portrait angled towards client. Casket and accessories catalogue with separate pricelist positioned to left of client – within sight and easy reach, but not in their face. *Little Book of Inspirational Verses*. The box of Carlton. He reached in the drawer for his can of Zesty Mint and fired two sharp bursts into his mouth. He pushed back his hair, breathed in deeply, and assumed position.

14

What the original architects of Eden Palm B&B lacked in talent, they had more than made up for in enthusiasm. It was a DIY project that had taken not only one bad wrong turn, but several. Starting life as a modest square face-brick home for a South African Railways employee, it had since transmogrified into a structure spanning several exotic architectural eras. Attached to the original clinker brick carcass was a series of protruding Bavarian turrets and other inspired flourishes of ill-defined nature. From here, it had wandered into the realm of Pretoria Tuscan, before taking a brief turn into Victorian in the form of a yellowing plastic broekie lace detail running the length of the veranda. According to the title deed, the previous owner had been a Mr GA van Staaten, who had purchased it with the proceeds of a retrenchment package from Zeerust Municipality. Mr van Staaten's relationship with his new home was short-lived, due to an unfortunate encounter with a poorly laid faux-Batavian tile that gifted him a shattered hip and concussion. In a display of uncharacteristic efficiency, Van Staaten's next-of-kin hired a private ambulance and promptly dispatched their father to a retirement home on the East Rand, where he passed his final days hovering between delirious delusions of grandeur and paranoid psychosis, thanks to a faulty morphine drip. In the interim, 13 Nerina Close was placed on auction and snapped up by one Otto Meissner.

Down the narrow passage and behind the locked door of Elephant Room, Steve Aldridge was already in bed, his head buried under the blanket. Safe in this makeshift womb, his befogged mind began to clear. Didn't accidents like this happen every day in South Africa? Yes, they did; the newspapers were full of them. In fact, he had read somewhere that a pedestrian was knocked over every three minutes. What difference then would one more make to the thousands already out there? It would soon be just another statistic in a mountain gathering dust in some government back office. Everybody knew the police couldn't be bothered with stuff like this; they had more important things to worry about. Aldridge didn't consider himself a racist by any stretch of the imagination – some of his best friends at work were black guys – but if he was coloured like Tarryn said, the South African Police Services would put less effort into the case. With something now positive to cling to, Aldridge dozed off.

A minute later a truck came crashing through the

bathroom wall and continued to idle. A door slammed, followed by a blinding flash of white fluorescent. Tarryn's face loomed large above him.

"What are you doing under there?"

"Just resting … You might need to jiggle the toilet handle to stop it from running."

"You think I didn't try that? Why don't you have a go, and while you're at it, you can get the hot water to work. It's not even lukewarm."

"Sorry, I was only trying to help."

"I bet the cheapskate hasn't even bothered to switch on the geyser." Tarryn pointed accusingly around the room. "And I bet everything here is from a second-hand junk shop." She sat down heavily on the single bed, triggering a mass protest from the springs below. "I hate this place!"

Sitting upright, Aldridge stretched his neck round to the left, then to the right. "It's only for one night, Tarryn. We've got to try make the best of a bad situation."

"Oh, really? Only one night? How then do you plan to get us out of here tomorrow?"

"What you mean?"

"As in, how are you going to fix the car?"

Aldridge hadn't yet managed to think that far ahead. "Well … I'll go find a garage first thing in the morning. We'll repair the radiator and be out of here by lunchtime."

"I hope you're right. Because this place is a shithole."

"Flipping hell, T! What if he hears you?" said Aldridge, scrambling off the bed and racing to shut the bathroom door.

"I don't care if he hears me. It's not like we're staying for free, you know."

Aldridge glanced nervously at the plywood drywalling separating their room from the main house. A thin shaft of light shone from the gap below. Tarryn dropped her towel to the floor and rummaged in her suitcase for a clean bra and panties; Aldridge looked the other way. She pulled on her tracksuit pants and T-shirt, plonked herself on the bed, and proceeded to file her nails as if her survival depended on it.

"Sorry, I'm just tired. It's been such a crappy day."

"Tell me about it." She was right, the place was a dump, but at least they had a bed to sleep in. Compared to the alternative – sleeping in the caravan, with a corpse in the car, or vice versa – it was paradise.

"Do you want me to pretend everything is fine and we're staying at Sun City? I can if you want?"

"No need to go that far." Aldridge reached behind his neck and explored the circumference of an angry pimple that had appeared from nowhere. "You can't deny your feelings. You feel what you feel."

Tarryn examined her hands. "My nails are such a mess."

"They look okay to me."

"You're just saying so … Don't you want to shower? You must be feeling all sweaty."

"I don't have the energy. I just want to rest."

"What are we going to do for supper?"

"I dunno. What do you want to do?"

"Also don't know, but we better eat something."

"I'm not even hungry."

"How about I micro the leftover ribs from last night and slice up some tomato and onion. We also have the garlic bread from the Spar that I can warm up."

"Sounds nice. What about the invite?"

"What invite?"

"You know, to join Mr Meissner and his wife for a free glass of sherry."

"I forgot about that. You go if you want, because I can't face it."

"Me too. But won't they think bad of us if we don't go?"

"Who cares if they do? I'm …" Tarryn had stopped filing her nails.

"Hell, T, what's wrong?" Aldridge moved across to his wife's bed and hugged her awkwardly. The tears were flowing freely down her face.

"What are we going to do, Stevie? We're not evil people. Why us? Why's this happening to us?"

Aldridge pulled his wife close to him. He could feel her warm wetness soaking through his Cape Union shirt, into his skin.

"I don't know. I don't know why. All I know is, I'm going to do whatever it takes to get us out of this mess."

15

Now that he had established the guy wasn't lying on ice, Truter was left with one of three possibles: 1. Gary Johnson was vrotting in the veld somewhere after suffering a heart attack-slash-stroke-diabetes poisoning. 2. Gary Johnson had left town in a hurry after pulling a fast one. 3. Gary Johnson was tucking into some fresh biefsteak on the side. Although Truter was still willing to bet his hard-earned cash on the latter, any policeman worth his salt kept an open mind.

With Meyer's Three Ships still floating in his bloodstream, he was in a reflective mood. As he had explained earlier to Delport, you couldn't rush a missing person's investigation. You had to be patient, allow the truth to marinate, and it would eventually reveal itself. But then again, what did Delport know about Zen and the Art of Police Investigation?

He leant across to the passenger seat and twisted the portable radio's dial until he found Drive Time with Vern. He cranked up the volume.

"Wat die fok?" Instead of Vernon Frost, some woman called Anel was coming at him. Truter pressed the accelerator into the floorboard; if you couldn't rely on your DJ to be there when you needed him, who then could you rely on?

The prospect of searching for a body had made the

missing person's case more interesting. This was right up his alley – real police work. If Johnson was in fact dead and vrotting in thirty-five-degree sun, it was just a matter of time before he found him, because Truter considered himself a seasoned expert in the area of Search and Recovery. He was no stranger to decomposing corpses, and had seen more than he could count in his career as a professional soldier. According to his mental calcs, the maggots and flies would soon be working their magic. The corpse would be blowing up like a balloon at a kid's party. The honk would be worse than a dead tortoise.

This Anel chick knew her music; he would grant her that. This was the real deal – music that cut like a knife deep into the soul. He cranked the volume higher, wound down the window, and handed himself over to the approaching deluge.

En my huis en my plaas tot kole verbrand
Sodat hulle ons kan vang
Maar daai vlamme en vuur
Brand nou diep, diep binne my.
De La Rey, De La Rey
Sal jy die Boere kom lei?
De La Rey, De La Rey
Generaal—

Truter slammed his hand against the radio, halting the advert for North West Nissan in its tracks. Wiping away the snot on his sleeve, he held down the clutch and coasted the van to a standstill at the side of the road. He sat for a minute, disoriented, staring straight ahead, pushing up against raw wounds.

He climbed out the van and scanned the terrain. Open African veld unfurled in all directions. The grass grew long under the power lines racing towards Witbank. He would never leave this country – they would have to kill him first.

A seasoned jackal sensing carrion on the African plain, Truter angled his head to one side and sniffed the thick afternoon air. He licked his finger and gauged the light breeze. He cocked his head downwind. He walked up and down the road, pitching his head this way and that, sampling the air, angling for the scent of putrefying flesh.

He waded into the grass. If Gary Johnson was turning sour in the veld somewhere between Brits and Edendal, he would eventually pick up the trail; if not today, tomorrow or the next day. Definitely within the next forty-eight hours. That much he knew from his days tracking Swapo.

Forcing a square peg into a round hole, Truter picked over Delport's statement. Assuming Bianca Reyneke – or whatever her name was – was telling the truth, the facts of the case could be summarised as follows: Her husband-slash-pomp partner had left the house at six hundred hours for his morning jog; at the time of his disappearance, he was wearing blue running shorts, a SAD vest, running shoes, and a Casio watch; he was in training for some half-marathon and had left his phone at home. According to the woman, he was usually back by seven hundred hours and at his place of work by eight hundred hours; he was presently employed in the services of Eden Palm B&B. By nine hundred hours, the chick became worried, and after searching for him for more than an hour, she drove to SAPS Edendal and opened a missing person's case.

Typical of Delport, the statement gave him near zilch to go on. If Johnson didn't pitch up soon, he would personally have to interrogate her. Several obvious questions sprung to mind:

1. Does your aforesaid husband/boyfriend/lover have a drinking problem?
2. Does he smoke dagga? Tik, mandrax, other?
3. Is your husband/boyfriend having an affair with another woman? If no, how do you know?
4. Is your husband then having an affair with another man? If no, how do you know?
5. Does your husband suffer from a mental illness? If no, do you suffer from a mental illness?
6. How many times has your husband/boyfriend gone AWOL before?
7. Have you been experiencing financial difficulties in the bedroom?
8. Have you been experiencing any other difficulties in the bedroom?
9. How many times a week/day do you and your husband/boyfriend—

The delicious images shaping in Truter's brain were cut short by the crackle of a distant police radio. He hurried back through the grass and reached into the window.

"Ja, Delport, what's up? ... Delport?"

"Sorry, sir. Just waiting again for you to say 'Over'. Over."

"What the ..." Truter twisted his head and spat into the ground. The slow pounding behind his eyes was coming back.

"Sorry for disturbing you, but I've just received a call from a Brigadier Duminy in Potchefstroom."

The hair on Truter's neck bristled. "So, what about it? Jissus, Delport, are you on tik? Slow down, man." The guy sounded like he was running a marathon.

"It seems Miss Reynold's father has connections in the force."

"Who the hell is Miss Reynolds?"

"Bianca Reynolds. The partner of Gary Johnson? The missing person, sir? Over."

"Okay, okay, I get it. And so? ... Delport!"

"Sorry, sir. The brigadier says we have to give the case priority status. That we must leave no stone unturned. And that from now on we must report directly to him."

"Is that a fact now?"

"Yes, sir. Those were his exact words."

"Well, that's very interesting indeed. Thank you, Delport."

"It's a pleasure, sir. Oh, before I forget, the rest of

that fax from Pretoria came in on the email." Truter's head throbbed with new intensity. Priority status. Poncy brigadiers from Potch. Missing person's. Faxes and emails coming at them non-stop. Pretoria sniffing up his arse for more stats. "I'm sure now it has to do with some undercover investigation, sir, because they're asking for a long, detailed checklist. Over."

"That's your department, Delport." The mere mention of checklist sat less comfortably with him than a Malema at a Freedom Front braai. Checklists meant one thing: admin, forms to fill, more useless waste of time.

"Not to worry, sir, I'm on it."

It never ceased to amaze Truter: Delport creaming himself at the prospect of filling in more forms.

"Good man. Delport?"

"Yes, sir? … Sorry, Over."

"Have you organised the SAPS display for the Agri Fest?"

"Almost there. I'm just waiting for the posters to be printed. Everything else is done."

"How big you making the posters?"

"A3, sir."

"White man's language, Delport. How big's that?"

"About the size of a half braai drum. The place you said we must use in Krugersdorp can't print them any bigger."

Truter had something way bigger in mind. Like highway billboard bigger. It was his best selfie yet – him at the shooting range, Sansui headphones on his head, the setting

North West sun reflecting off his mirror sunglasses, the barrel of his gun pointing into the camera. It would be nothing less than inspiring to the kids of today, the crime fighters of tomorrow. He should have done the job himself. Sent the picture to one of the big companies in Joburg.

"Alright, but make sure you print enough of them. Now, anything else on your mind, Delport?"

"I think that's all for now, sir."

"Good. In that case … Whoa, hold your horses, Delport, I've just spotted something." Leaving the police radio to dangle by its cord, Truter walked back into the veld, and picked up the dusty takkie lying on the ground. Holding it by the laces, he carried it back to the van. "You said the guy was wearing running shoes?"

"Who, sir?"

"The flipping missing person, idiot. In your report, you said he was wearing running shoes, yes or no?"

"Yes, sir. According to Miss Reynolds—"

"I bet you didn't bother asking what make they were?"

"I actually did. They were Nikes. Size nine, if I remember right. You want me to double-check the statement, sir? Over."

Truter pulled open the laces. Jackpot! "Constable Delport, for once I'm impressed with your police work."

16

After a fairly long and mediocre life, Glen Mitchell appeared to have gone quietly. Other than for the glistening trickle of saliva running from the corner of his mouth, down the left side of his chin, into his collar and lower into his shirt, where it had ended in a dark pool framed by the E of Castle and L of Lager, there wasn't much evidence he had moved on to the next world at all.

On the far side of the La-Z-Boy, Pastor Gerald Phelps stifled a yawn. His day had been long and tiring, and it was high time he brought proceedings to a head. Fashioning a steeple with the tips of his fingers, he kicked into gear.

"A lovely man, a truly lovely man." Phelps allowed a moment of reflective silence, before continuing. "Mrs Mitchell, I know you want nothing but the best for your husband. Am I right?"

"Yes, of course," the woman whispered.

"Excellent. That's what we all want for Glen. Why? Because he deserves the best!" Phelps cleared his throat. "Now, with regard to certain logistic issues pertaining—"

"You're very kind."

"Not at all, it's the least I can do. Here you go." Phelps peeled off a Kleenex and handed it to the woman. "First things first ... If I may, I would like to arrange for New Horizons to take care of Glen's further needs." He held up his hands. "Of course, I know you might have someone else in mind, but I don't think you want to deal with these fly-by-nights. Just not worth the risk, Mrs Mitchell." He reached into his pocket. "'New Horizons is our name. Customer service is our game.' Very professional business card, don't you think? No, you keep it. These are good operators, Mrs Mitchell. Been in the business for yonks, and still owner-run. That says something in my book."

"Thank you. I appreciate the recommendation."

"Just doing my job." Phelps looked past the woman, through the Trelli, contemplating the evening ahead. "Because I don't want you to worry, I've already organised with New Horizons." He looked at his watch. "In fact, they should be here any minute. That's what I call service with a capital S. Not like those fly-by-nights that keep you waiting forever and a day. Been there, done that, Mrs Mitchell … Mrs Mitchell?"

Doreen Mitchell was no longer present. Phelps reached over the cooling corpse and gave her shoulder a reassuring squeeze. His phone vibrated in his pocket.

"Sorry about this … Looks like they're running a few minutes late, but no worries, I promise they'll be here soon." Phelps snapped the phone shut and pulled on his collar. It was time to get moving. "Well, looks like my job is done here for now, so how about I phone you first thing tomorrow so we can talk through the funeral arrangements?"

Doreen Mitchell nodded gratefully. "Thank you. For everything."

"May the Lord give you strength, Mrs Mitchell."

And with this, Pastor Gerald Phelps shimmied from the sitting room and out the front door.

Her face still registering the silent shock of sudden loss, Doreen Mitchell seated herself in the wingback opposite her dead husband, crossed her hands on her lap, and waited for the people from New Horizons. The Sanyo clock above the TV flashed five forty-five. After a while, she peered up at Glen. He was as she had found him on her return from bowls: his eyes still glued to the now silent Telefunken he had devoted a large part of his life to, his head tilted slightly back, his mouth open in what was either a final gasp or final cheer – it was hard to tell. The contents of a half-eaten bowl of peanuts and raisins lay scattered about him like confetti. Pieces of nut and other stringy bits were stuck between his teeth. His face and neck were blue. A deep shade of crimson blue, the likes of which she had never seen before.

17

Profiled against the setting sun twenty kilometres west of Edendal, Clifford Abrahams fumbled for his zip, and with barely a moment to spare let loose with a golden torrent.

"Sweet baby Jesus," he crooned. He arched back, hands

behind his head, swinging his manhood from side to side. There was nothing like a good piss in nature – it ran a close second to a good boskak.

For a moment back there, he'd been seriously worried he was going to wet himself in the guy's Interlink truck. But like his stepdad used to say, if you're batting on a good wicket, suck it for all it's worth. Rides like that didn't come along every day – eight hours non-stop, with a free Steers burger and Grape Fanta chucked in along the way. At the rate he was going, he would hit Durban first thing in the morning; his boet and Tracy were going to be super surprised when he knocked on their door. He could already taste the ice-cold Blackie with his name on it.

Squeezing out the last drops, Cliffie opened his eyes and packed away his love weapon into its holster. He rubbed the dribble spot – it had to be an age thing. He sucked in the late afternoon air and surveyed the open veld stretching in every direction, broken by the flat koppies in the far distance. It was something out of a cowboy fliek.

"Africa, you beauty!" Cliffie shouted into the dying day. He dug into his back pocket and pulled out his G-Shock – the strap had sheared off months back. A gnawing urgency took hold. As much as he loved being in Mother Africa's bosom, he had little desire to spend another night with her.

Hoisting up his suitcase, Cliffie started walking. Someone would eventually feel sorry for him; they always did. Especially around sunset – hitchhiker's golden hour,

Norm had called it, when drivers felt most guilty for abandoning you to the night. It was a known scientific fact.

Cliffie stopped and gazed up and down the road. Not a car in sight. He carried on walking. What he wouldn't do for an ice-cold one, with a free bowl of peanuts and raisins on the side. Chased down by a juicy sirloin swimming in pepper sauce and Spur onion rings and chips. He stepped up the pace. The day was turning red; there was no ways he was sleeping a second night in the veld.

According to the trucker, it was less than fifteen kays to the next town. Cliffie stared up ahead, regrouping his thoughts; he would keep walking until he found a spot for a car to pull off easily. It wasn't like the old days when drivers would reverse down the M1 highway to give him a lift. Nowadays you had to give them a flipping runway. He continued walking. And then halted.

Something silver and glittery had caught his eye in the grass. Not one to pass up an opportunity – even if it was just a Coke can chucked from a car – he abandoned his suitcase and waded into the veld.

"Now, what do we have here, good sir?"

Laid out neatly on the ground, as if someone had just sommer put it there, a SOS bracelet – same as the one his brother used to wear for his homophilia, or whatever it was he suffered from. Puzzled, Cliffie looked to the left, then to the right, expecting its owner to appear from the bush any second. No owner forthcoming, he scooped up the bracelet, spat on the tag and gave it a quick polish against his sleeve, then held it up to the dying light.

GARY JOHNSON
TYPE 1 DIABETES
ON INSULIN PUMP
ALGYS: MORPHINE
ICE 054-526 6697

Hoping for more of the same – like a wallet filled with cash, for instance – Cliffie passed another minute expanding the search zone. Coming up empty handed, he turned his attention back to the bracelet; it had to be worth a few bucks at a pawn shop, and might even be silver. He stuffed it into his trouser pocket and made his way back up to the road. Time was ticking, it was starting to get dark, and Cliffie Abrahams was starting to get edgy. It was time to hit the city lights.

18

EXAS GRILL – the neon "T" had long since thrown in the towel – was squeezed between the Joshua Doore and Happy Cash Loans. A security gate with a buzzer barred the entrance. The shop front windows were draped in louvered blinds, the floor was grey Show Floor, the lighting was fluorescent – in a past life Texas Grill had served as Edendal Isuzu.

Occupying a round table at the centre of the restaurant, a group of elderlies from nearby Tuis Huis hunched over a fixed menu of meat stew, rice, and creamed spinach. A sales rep in a polyester shirt and navy-blue pants sat at the table opposite, nervously checking his phone. At the far end of the bar, two middle-aged males with sunburnt necks nursed Red Heart rum and Coke. Above them, a squadron of flies orbited lazily under the ceiling fan.

Tucked into his booth, Clinton Truter reached for the bottle of Chateau and topped up his glass. Working his toothpick, he tracked Toni's new waitress – one of those circles-around-the-eyes types who had been through life's ringer. Not that he would say no to the bod; if and when it came to it, he'd cover her face with the South African flag and do it for his country.

Truter poked at a chip caked in a drying scab of tomato sauce, thought better of it, and pushed the plate away. What he needed was a smoke. He raised his hand to the sky and caught the waitress's attention. Tight T-shirts and jeans did it for him, even on a chick whose face would soon look like a dried prune. Just as he thought, no wedding ring.

"How was your T-bone?"

"Lekker. You want to organise me a ashtray?"

"Sure. You want the two-for-one in a doggy bag, or you going to have it now?

"Chuck it in a body bag, I'll have it for breakfast."

"Same as before – bloody and bleating?"

"You got it, girlie."

The waitress smiled grimly. "Anything else?"

"Coffee."

"Nescafe or filter?"

"If you can't go big, go home. Nescafe. And I want it like my women, okay?"

"Ja, ja. Black and strong."

"No, white and weak." Truter cackled. He was getting somewhere with this chick; he could feel the vibe between them. "One momento, senora." His phone was vibrating on the table. His mom. He pressed "Decline" – whatever it was, she could wait.

"I'll get your ashtray and coffee in the meantime."

"And one of Toni's Greek biscuits while you're at it. By the way, what's your handle?"

"Deirdre."

She didn't ask him his. Playing hard to get. He liked that.

Truter settled comfortably into the booth, following Deirdre's arse to the bar. The rate he was going, she'd be spreading for him in no time. He took a sip of Chateau, altogether content with how the day was ending. He had turned it around, taken charge of it. As he had so often explained to Delport, it was all about having the right Attitude.

He had made up his mind: from here on, he would work with Pretoria, Duminy, whoever. No problem. Not only would he find and deliver Mr VIP Gary Johnson on a tray, dead or alive, or any other missing person on their Priority Status list, he would give Pretoria their stats and anything else they threw at him. If Delport was right, if the stats were part of something big going down, he wanted in on the action. If he played his cards right, this was the stuff promotions were made of.

"Gracias, Deirdre. And you remembered my ashtray. Not just a … pretty face, hey."

Truter reached for the sugar bowl and tore open two sachets. He stirred his coffee and took a sip. Added another two. More like it. Dr Santos couldn't even pronounce the word diabetes. Pulling hard on his Pall Mall and aiming a smoke ring at the ceiling, Truter saw a new future unfolding before him …

He saw himself walking down the aisle of a packed hall, the crazy clapping as he stepped up to the podium to accept his Exemplary Service Award from the Minister of Police. They would want him to make a speech; he would have to think about what to say. After that, who knows, the world would be his oyster. He could become one of those motivational speakers, travelling around the country, speaking to unmotivated members of the force – Delport, for example – to get them off their poepols and back on the street where they were needed most. He saw the free hotels; the room service; the mini bottles of whisky on the aeroplane; the Kulula air hostesses – he'd heard they were hornier than nurses – the strangers coming up to him in the street, thanking him for returning law and order to the country, allowing them to sleep secure. After that, he would settle down and write a book and the bucks would flow in big time. He had been threatening for a long time to write a book about his life and experiences – this would be his chance. *Smashing the International Cartels*, by Clinton Truter … General Clinton Truter. It had a nice ring to it. The book would be used as a study aid by Interpols across—

Only now had he noticed the two pissing it up at the bar. There was something about the scrawny one with the hyena laugh. The angle of the head, the silver-grey hair Brylcreamed back, the panel-beaten face when he turned to the side. Why did he know that laugh—

And then it hit him like a pickaxe handle on the back of the head: Freddie fokken Ferreira!

How long had it been? Twenty, twenty-five years since he'd last set eyes on the guy? He had to now be in his fifties – same as him. Besides the silver hair, Freddie still looked the same. Same slimy operator written all over the face. Same gift-of-the-gabber who could sell a Hilux bakkie of sand to ISIS.

Heart racing, Truter peered through the gap in the vinyl headrest. Freddie's drinking buddy also now looked disturbingly familiar. Heavy bones, six-two-plus, skin on his neck burnt black, dressed to kill in his Agri-special khaki pants and camo bush hat. The guy turned sideways to say something to Freddie. Truter jolted.

He had thought Dippies was long dead and buried. The

face was fleshier and the body thicker around the edges, but it was one and the same Dippies as in the faded photo lying around in a shoe box somewhere – of him and the rest of them going ape around the fire after a Swapo contact.

Truter stared hard at the smouldering stompie in the ashtray, trying to pull himself right. Time had yanked up the handbrake and done a U-turn on him. Present had dissolved into past.

Deirdre walked over and cleared his table. The people from the retirement home shuffled out in single file. The sales rep headed to the bogs. The Leopards trailed twelve-zero to the Crusaders on the flatscreen. Toni walked past him with a silver baking tray heaped with burger patties. The lift music stopped playing. Truter registered none of it.

Without warning, Ferreira pushed back his barstool, stood up and zipped up his jacket. Tossing back the remains of his glass, Dippenaar adjusted his bush hat and followed Ferreira into the street, forcing Truter deeper into the red vinyl. His heart was pumping on overdrive as the two passed by the window. Ferreira walked over to the blue Camry parked under the EXAS GRILL sign and returned with a package. He handed it to Dippenaar, slapped him on the shoulder, and walked back to his car. Dippenaar turned and crossed the road to the double cab parked opposite. He climbed in, revved the engine and tailed Freddie out the car park. The cars swung a right into

Hoof, then disappeared into the night.

Truter sat up slowly. His hand still shaking, he reached for the Chateau.

19

"What did you say your name was, again?"

"Abrahams, sir. Clifford James Abrahams. I would give you a business card if I hadn't left them in my car with my wallet." Cliffie slapped his forehead. "I'm such a moron."

"No worries, my friend, you look kaput. Have a sitdown on the couch. You want my wife to get you something to drink? Coffee? Tea? Juice?"

Cliffie sat down wearily, chased by a dramatic sigh. He pulled out his hanky and proceeded to mop his face. "I won't lie to you people, it's been a hell of a day. I don't usually drink, but right now I wouldn't say no to something stronger."

"What you need is a stiff sherry."

Cliffie peered over the hanky. "I wouldn't even say no to a whisky. That's how bad it is."

"Consider it done, sir. I've got some nice Three Ships going. Single or double?"

"A double would be … Ag, make it a triple; I don't want you jumping up and down for me. Check my hands, Mrs Meissner, they're still shaking." Cliffie sank deeper into the couch, luxuriating in the corduroy. "You people are very kind."

"It's the least we can do," said Susan Meissner.

"Straight or on the rocks, sir?"

"I don't want to put you out; straight is perfect."

"Come join me at the bar, Mr Abrahams."

Susan Meissner stood up. "And I will leave you men to talk."

Taking up poll position behind the pine counter, Otto Meissner handed Cliffie his drink, and poured himself a sherry. "Gesundheit and all that jazz. So, my friend, tell me some more about your Galactic Tours thingie."

Taking a hefty slug, Cliffie swallowed hard. He licked his lips. This was seriously good stuff. Better than he'd tasted in a long time. If he played his cards right, there could be more where it came from.

"Galactic Tours? Oh, yes … As I was saying before your wife came in, I'm what you call a global accommodation scout. GAS, for short. So … my job is to find quality B&Bs for our overseas clients."

"And, how's business going?"

"You won't believe the demand. Our databases are chock-a-block with foreigners looking for quality, for … for something different." Cliffie peered over the rim of his glass. So far, so good. All the old *Getaway* and Kulula magazines he'd read during his stint at Pollsmoor were coming into good use. He took another gulp, aware of the man's beady eyes watching him. "Very, very nice."

"There's more where it came from, my friend. When you say 'quality', what is it you mean?"

"Well … let's take your place here. My clients would go mad for it."

"Is that a fact now?"

"One hundred per cent. The foreigners are tired of staying in the same old five-star hotels … They are tired of being served by the same old human robots."

"That's very interesting to hear, because I was telling the wife the same thing just the other day. The tourists want character. Am I right?"

"Exactly! You've hit the hammer on its head. Character is what they're after." Cliffie held out his empty glass. "I won't say no. Same again is perfecto."

"Enjoy it, my friend, because I like what you're saying."

The Three Ships was fast going to Cliffie's head. Equally matched by an uptick in confidence. "Character. That is a good word. My foreigner clients want character. They want to meet the real people. Not the phonies behind the reception desk. And let me tell you, it's not just the Brits, or the whatisnames … the Frenchies and Germans. It's everyone. Even the Japs and Chinese. They're also sick and tired of hotels. In fact, I'll let you in on a secret." Meissner leant in closer. Cliffie screwed his finger into the bar counter. "This is where the future lies!"

Meissner sipped his sherry. "All quite fascinating, Mr Abrahams. I've told the wife for years it's not about how many channels you have on the TV, or the fancy soaps and lotions next to the bath, or the extra blankets on the bed, or ... or fancy cups and plates, or rubbish like that. What you're telling me is that people are looking for a unique experience. Something they don't get at home. Not so?"

"Exactly," said Cliffie, monitoring the flushed face opposite, the darting tongue. He had to be careful with this one.

"Where did you say you broke down?"

Cliffie wiped his mouth with the back of his hand. "Ag, must be about sixty kays from here. The worst part, because of the stress and all, I went and forgot my briefcase in the boot. Can you believe that?"

"It could happen to anyone. Where's the car now?"

"My company has already organised with Avis in Joburg to fetch it and bring me a new one."

"All the way from Johannesburg?"

"They must do what they must do." With the whisky working its magic, Cliffie felt back on solid ground. "We don't mess around. They'll send a helicopter if I tell them to."

"They would do *that* for you? I'm impressed."

Cliffie drained the dregs. "Oh, ja. Not that they'll do it this time, but it happens quite often. It all depends on ... what we call access." As per Cliffie's God-given talent for making connections where no logical connections previously existed, the TV series *Skattejag* floated into mental view. "Once I was working in the Alps mountains, hunting for something unique for a rich client of ours—"

"Like ski lodges and things?"

"Exactly. Ski lodges and things. Huge demand. Anyways, there was an avalanche higher up. Not a huge one, but we were trapped at our lodge because the roads below were covered over. I lie to you not, less than two hours later I hear the company chopper coming over the mountain. Even I was impressed."

Meissner jammed his tongue into the bottom of the sherry glass. "Incredible. We need to talk more, my friend, because I've got some big ideas for this place that I'd like to squeeze your brain over."

Seizing the moment – like Norm would have said, it was all in the timing – Cliffie placed his glass on the counter and stood up. "Anytime, sir, but looks like I better start making a move—"

"Where do you think you're going this time of the night?"

Cliffie flashed his worried look. "Isn't there a hotel or something close by?"

"This is it, my friend. Which means you are our guest until your replacement car arrives."

Cliffie flashed another worried look. "But what about payment? I saw on the board outside—"

Meissner sneered. "What board? You can settle up when you get your wallet. How's that sound?"

"I don't know what to say—"

"Don't look so surprised. You're about to experience Austro-African hospitality at its best," gloated Meissner.

"What can I say, sir? I am grateful. And I am humbled."
Cliffie scratched around in his head for something to add.
Something to seal the deal. "I don't know why, but I've
got this funny feeling you and me are going to do some
good business together."

Otto Meissner reached over the bar and pumped Cliffie's
hand. "I think so too, my friend."

Day 2

20

Steve Aldridge jolted awake to barking outside the window and a fly circling above his head. A blade of light cut through the rip in the curtain. He eyed the Casio G-Shock on the bedside table: five thirty-five. His wife was sprawled across the other single bed. Her arm flopped loosely over the side. Piglet-on-teat sounds gurgled from her open mouth.

Corkscrewing painfully onto his back, Aldridge contemplated the brown stain on the ceiling – all he saw in it was dried blood at a grisly murder scene. He pulled the pillow over his face, with little effect – the recent events still came at him like ravenous sewer rats.

Aldridge faced his first crossroad of the day: Do nothing and enjoy a nervous breakdown, or, execute … go along with Tarryn's grand plan. She had it all worked out. One: take the car in first thing and get the radiator fixed or welded, "or whatever"; it only had to get them to

Kruger. Two: offload *him* somewhere – in the veld, "or wherever" – on their way to Kruger. Three: continue as per normal with their holiday, so that people wouldn't get suspicious.

According to the plan, by midday there would be two hundred kays between them and the nightmare. By evening they would be sitting around the fire enjoying sundowners and snacks. By the next morning they would start forgetting. That's what humans did – they forgot. By the time they got back to Sasolburg, life would have returned to normal, as if nothing had ever happened.

With something to hold onto, Aldridge lapsed into a calm stupor. The fly had shifted its focus to Tarryn. With detached interest, he watched it settle on her face and hop across to the wet patch at the corner of her mouth. An arm came up and swatted the air. The fly circled back and settled on her chin.

He sat up and studied the pair of white feet on the salt-and-pepper carpet; they seemed oddly disconnected from his body. His gut felt heavy under his T-shirt. His neck and shoulders ached. It was time to kick into action.

Careful not to wake the sleeping tiger, Aldridge gathered up his clothes from the floor and dressed quietly. He dug his Rockies from under the bed and tiptoed to the door. He unlocked it and stepped into the day.

The sweet smell of Epol hovered on the morning air, punctuated by a trail of fresh chocolate turd clusters on the cement path. Navigating the minefield, Aldridge made his way along the side of the house. An open sliding door lay to the front of him. Short machine gun bursts of what sounded like German combined with English punctured the drawn curtain. Keeping his head low, Aldridge slunk past.

Peering around the corner, he scanned for Adolf's whereabouts. With the coast clear, he proceeded cautiously down the driveway. More than anything he needed to get out into the open and clear his head. Regroup. Get perspective. Focus on getting the job done. There was something to be taken from this whole thing. A life lesson. It wasn't like it looked on the surface; you always had choices. Reality was all in the mind.

The early morning sun on his face, and Adolf nowhere in sight, Aldridge felt a flutter of renewed hope. From now on he would focus on what mattered in life. His career. His relationship. His health. He would rejoin the gym, lose a couple of kilos, muscle up on those Verimark protein shakes, start jogging before work. He would sign up for Dale Carnegie Advanced: Mastering Your Destiny in this Life and the Next. "Bootcamp for the soul" was how the brochure described it. He would—

He had come face to face with a heavy-duty chain with Viro lock and a fence designed to keep in game of the long-horned variety. He looked up, played out the scenario, and decided against it – it wasn't called razor wire for nothing. He pushed against the gate and his rising desperation; neither budged. He stared through the mesh.

His Fortuner and his Jurgens and what remained of his freedom beckoned from under the blue gum trees.

Aldridge squinted into the sun … and pushed the thought from his mind. Even a school kid knew shadow and light combined to create weird effects. Even so … Again, he dismissed the thought. His mouth now inexplicably dry, his heart pumping in his throat, he walked along the fence line, stopped, glanced back. It couldn't be. Or could it? Shadow or no shadow, it was staring him in the face – the caravan door, hanging wide open for all the world to see.

21

Clinton Truter stood up in the bath and pulled the window shut; the brats from number 12 were messing big time with his mojo. Settling back in the water, he picked up where he'd left off – giving it to Deidre the waitress on his kitchen floor. Until a few seconds ago, she'd been loving it: wet as a spons and begging for more.

Truter hit the Rewind on the mental tape, back to where he had offered to give her a lift home after her shift at EXAS GRILL. The van wasn't even out the carpark and she was telling him straight out that she wanted him bad – she knew it from the moment she saw him. And what with her own messy divorce, she wasn't into the romantic wining-and-dining thing; all she wanted was hot Grade A beef. Which suited him just fine. He also didn't have time for complication.

Doing his best to ignore the snivelling outside his bathroom window, Truter upped the tempo. He had Deirdre moaning on the linoleum, her brown hair splayed in a fan. He could see himself reflected in the oven door, giving it to her hard. No ways she was faking the moaning like Sharon used to do; this one knew SAB quality when she got it. He was doing his best to satisfy, but what with his sore knee, the caretaker and Mrs Jacobs from 205 now having a fat chinwag in the passage, and the thing with Ferreira and Dippenaar still fresh on his mind, Truter was taking strain. Worst of all, he'd hit a nail on the road and was running soft. With time against him, he pressed down hard on the clutch and switched gear, giving it to Deidre on a blanket in the back of the police van. But even that wasn't working.

Conceding defeat, Truter pulled the plug and climbed out the bath and dried himself off. He walked through to the sitting room and turned up the TV. For a while now, he'd been wanting to phone in for one of those black blow-up mattress deals. He could see Deidre sliding around on one, smeared in baby oil, and for a moment contemplated getting it up again for her and her nympho cousin. But the day was ticking, and what with Ferreira and Dippenaar chewing on his brain, he was no longer in the mood.

Truter walked over to the laundry basket and scratched

around for a pair of jocks with another day or two left in them. He pulled them on and headed into the kitchen, where his T-bone takeaway was waiting in the microwave. Turning the dial to Turbo, he stared absently at the meat revolving slowly under the yellow light, his head back at that night with Jakkals and the others on the Farm.

22

"More coffee, sir?"

The sales rep held out his cup. "Thanks, my friend."

"Hundred per cent Nescafe Gold is what you're drinking there." Otto Meissner hooked a thumb in the direction of the couple in the corner. "Not the overrated stuff these city slickers pay big bucks for. Cappuccino, Frappuccino, café latte … Suzy, what they call that biscuit they serve with it?"

"Biscotti."

"Yes, biscotti. They give you this tiny biscotti biscuit, some shaving cream on top, then think they can charge an arm and a leg." Meissner tapped his head. "You want my opinion? Bonkers!"

"I hear you loud and clear," said the rep, flashing a gold incisor, and lifting his cup to Meissner. "You don't get better than this."

Meissner sidled over to the Aldridge table. "More toast

for you people?"

"No, thank you, I'm banting," said the wife.

"What, like you training for badminton?"

Susan Meissner gave a nervous laugh from behind the buffet table. "It's a diet where you can't eat bread and pasta, am I right?"

"Yes, but instead of the carbs we can eat a lot of animal fats and protein—"

"I see you've hardly touched your plate, sir; I suppose then you're also into this banting smanting?"

"I'm just not feeling so good. I think I must have—"

"Steve's got a little stomach bug, that's all. You want me to eat your bacon, sweetie?"

Otto Meissner edged closer, angling for a glimpse of cleavage. "You want my opinion? It's just another one of those diet crazes that will come and will go."

"Maybe they don't want your opinion, Otto. Sorry, guys … Can I get you some more milk, Mrs Aldridge?"

"Just a drop. Actually, banting isn't a diet, it's a way of life. That's what Dr Tim Noakes calls it."

"Who is Dr Tim Noakes?"

"The scientist who discovered banting."

"Banting discovered banting, Steve. Dr Tim Noakes just imported it into this country. He's one of those super-bright genius types with a hundred titles behind his name." Tarryn Aldridge reached across and removed the crust from her husband's plate. "What is the plan with those tiles in the corner?"

"Don't bring up the war," said Susan Meissner, clearing the empty plate, and giving her husband a hard look across the table.

"What you mean?"

"The guy who was supposed to lay them for us hasn't pitched."

"He's probably sick or something?"

"That's what I said."

Otto Meissner tugged irritably at his goatee. "So sick he can't even pick up a phone, Suzy? So sick he ignores my calls? How many so far? Five? Ten? Fifteen? You know what it's costing me? Rule number one: never listen to a woman for—"

"Otto! Sorry, guys—"

"I'm just saying." whined Meissner.

"Well, don't."

"Maybe we should change the subject … You want me to help you with your sausage, Stevie?"

Meissner waited until his wife had returned to the kitchen, then maneuvered behind Mrs Aldridge for a deeper look-in. "This is what happens when you're too generous. It's not like where I come from in Austria where people respect one another. Here? Pfft! Nobody respects nobody." He aimed an accusing finger at the pile of Tuscan Sunset tiles in the corner. "I felt sorry for this character. I took him off the street, gave him a second chance at life, taught him everything I know. If it wasn't for me …" Meissner's face had turned puffy and red and sweaty. His left eye twitched. "Two days, not a word. Nothing! Zilch!" Meissner breathed out slowly. "Him and me had an agreement."

"I'm on your page, my friend," said the sales rep from across the room. "There's no respect any more in this country."

Otto Meissner smiled gratefully. "At long last, someone who understands where I'm coming from."

"One hundred per cent. People like us must stand together. Ons moet saam staan. Show these lui gatte who's boss!"

"A man after my own heart, Mr Ferreira. How about I fetch you some more coffee?"

"I won't say no."

The Aldridges stood up from their table. "Thanks for breakfast, Mrs Meissner."

"Only a pleasure. You guys have a good day now."

Susan Meissner pulled the door behind the couple. "Is my husband still carrying on about those stupid tiles?"

But Otto Meissner wasn't quite done. "With you as my witness, Mr Ferreira—"

"I'm really sorry about this. Otto, please—"

"No worries, ma'am. A man must say what a man must say."

"Thank you, sir. With you as my witness, let me just say one thing to my wife here.

"Okay, Otto, what is it?"

"Gary Johnson mustn't for one second think he can step a foot back on my property. That's it, that is all I have to say."

23

Delport's Corsa was already there when Truter pulled into the station yard. Typical subordinate behaviour: always trying to get the one up on their superiors. Truter pushed the thought aside. Like it said on the Wimpy sugar sachet: *Live today like it's your last.* Not even Delport and his silly mind games were going to mess it up. Truter had read his Bible verses. He had swallowed his pills. He had eaten a T-bone for breakfast. He had taken a good crap. He felt calm and collected.

Truter parked the van and slammed the door. Sidestepping the alcoholic rubbishes and their vuil babies sucking on empty, he rolled up the cement stairs to the charge office.

"Good morning, South Africa!" he boomed. "Delport, waar is jy!"

Constable Delport appeared from behind the kitchenette curtain, carrying a plastic jug. "Morning, Sergeant. How's it going?"

"Top of the pops. Where you taking that?"

"The plants at the front are looking a bit thirsty—"

"Chrissake, Delport. Here our motherland is burning, and you're watering your daisies. Just make sure nobody sees you; you'll give the police services a bad name. I hope you switched the kettle on whilst you were in there?"

"Just boiled, sir."

"Nice. At least you got your priorities straight. What you waiting for? Go water your daisy flowers and then let's drink some serious coffee. Whose turn was it anyway to bring the biscuits?"

"Yours, I think?" ventured Delport.

"You bullshitting me again?"

"But there are still some Lemon Creams left over from yesterday," Delport quickly added.

"There we go. I knew there was a reason I didn't buy."

Truter swaggered into his office. It sat to the side of the charge counter, with a direct view over the front entrance – what with ISIS working its way down Africa, one had to be hyper-vigilant. The Taliban café owner around the corner was a case in point; he didn't trust him further than he could shoot a load.

Truter reached into the filing cabinet for his Ricoffy. An unopened roll of toilet paper was perched alongside. "Now, where were you when I needed you, my lovely?" he crooned. The memory was still raw, as was his ring rash. The Vaseline hadn't kicked in yet, and for all he knew, carbon paper contained toxic chemicals. How was he going to explain the blue dye to Dr Santos? A bridge he would cross later, because right now he would kill for a cup of coffee and rusk. He gave the Ouma box a shake. Empty. He could have sworn there were some left last time he looked. If Delport wanted a rusk, why didn't he just ask? Instead of snooping around his office, helping himself to his property. What he needed was one of those

Verimark home security cameras—

Delport was standing at the door, holding a mug. "Here you go, sir."

"Now we're talking, Delport! How many sugars you put in?"

"Only four. Like you said."

"Since when do you listen to me? It's all horseskak. You go to one quack and he says you've got type two diabetes. You go to another and now all of a sudden you've got type one. Who do you believe, Delport? Quack one or quack two?"

"Don't know, sir."

"None of them, that's who. Especially if it's one of those Cuban commies flooding the market. You do know why they're here?"

"Not exactly."

"Because they can't get a job in their own country. And you know why they can't get a job?"

"Because of unemployment in their home country?"

"No. Because they're not qualified, that's why!" Truter tapped his temple. "You have to use this, Delport. It's called logic thinking." He drew an imaginary line across the floor. "That's why I am here, and you are there. You sure you put in four sugars? I can hardly taste it." He cocked his head to one side. "Am I imagining it, or did you say Lemon Cream?"

"Oh, ja. I'll go fetch them."

"Fantastico. And then I say we get off our poepols and

do some graft for a change. What you say to that?"

Truter shook the last Lemon Cream from the pack. He took a slurp from his Good Morning Handsome mug, swirling the contents back and forth, savouring the Lemon-Ricoffy sensation.

"Carry on, Delport?"

"I was just saying, it's incredible you finding Mr Johnson's running shoe in the veld."

"Nothing incredible about it. It's what we call normal police work." Truter lifted the mug, draining the dregs, and immediately regretting it. There was only one thing worse than cold coffee: cold coffee mixed with sludge of Lemon Cream.

"What's the next step from here? Must I inform the family?"

"Don't be crazy, man. Next thing they'll want to know where the other shoe and the rest of him are. We don't want to give them false hopes. It's simple, Delport. We first find the guy, dead or alive, then we inform them."

"I understand, sir, but it's just that Brigadier Duminy keeps phoning. I thought maybe we could give them something to show we are working on it."

"What the! Does the Potch toss think I sit on my gat watching TV all day? Stuff him, Delport. He gets his missing person when he gets his missing person. You understand me?"

"I understand."

"Good." Truter stared into the bottom of his mug. "So what else is on the slab?"

"Pretoria also phoned." Truter clamped down on his jaw. Now what did they want from him? Forever breathing down his neck, watching, waiting, hunting for the jugular. "Sir, I might be wrong, but I'm more and more convinced there's an undercover investigation going on." Truter's guts tightened. What were they investigating undercover? So-called police brutality? Nowadays you had to offer your suspect tea and a slice of milk tart before interrogating him. It had become so bad you weren't allowed to lay a finger on them if they didn't cooperate. For fok sakes, whose side was the Commissioner of Police on anyway? "Sir?"

"Carry on, I'm listening."

"The way I see it, there's a connection between the stats they've been asking us for and the investigation."

"And what might that connection be, Delport? Besides your overactive imagination."

"Well, it's just the type of stats. They are very specific and—"

"Like what?" Truter was already regretting his decision to work with head office on this one. If it weren't for the prospect of tucking into a juicy Kulula air hostess …

Delport wiped his superior's coffee dribble off the fax paper. "Like, for instance they want a breakdown of our mortality records by MVAs, pedestrian accidents, deaths in the home, death by natural causes … that type of thing.

And then for each of these they want the specifics. Time of death, exact location, race, sex, age, employment status, insurance policy details, which we don't have. Maybe you want to take a look?"

Truter leant across and patted his deputy on the shoulder. "Delport, do I look like I have time to waste on this rubbish? It's your baby. You and your paperwork, it's no wonder you don't get anything done." He clicked his fingers. "What else you got for me today?"

"Just a small petty crime issue," said Delport, reaching under the counter.

"No such thing as petty crime, and don't you forget it. Today's petty criminal is tomorrow's mass murderer!"

Delport moved on quickly. "Jan Dissel was found drunk and disorderly wearing this K-Way jacket."

"The little bliksem." Truter hated to admit it but he had become oddly fond of the Dissel brothers. Not that his affection prevented him in any way from applying the full force of the law. "Where's he now?"

"Working off his babalaas in the cell. He must have taken some bad stuff, because he's been carrying on non-stop about a dead white man in a caravan."

"That's the Blue Train talking, Delport. It methes with your brain. Get it? 'Methes' with your brain? I should have been a bladdy comedian. You know how much those guys make? Mega bucks."

"We could try track down the owner of the jacket, because it comes from one of those Cape Union Mart stores you find in the cities." Delport peeled back the collar. "It has the name SJ Aldridge."

"You checked the pockets?"

"Yes, sir. The only thing was a cash receipt from a Wagon Wheels in Krugersdorp. You think it belongs to a tourist?"

"Maybe. Maybe not. But who cares, anyway? If it's a tourist he's already doer and gone. Did that cross your mind? No, it didn't, Delport. What size is it?"

"Large."

Pity, thought Truter. There was no ways he would fit into a Large. "Give me the jacket, because I know exactly what you're thinking. You're thinking if Sergeant Truter can sniff out a missing person's takkie in the veld, he can then sniff out a SJ Aldridge. Not so, Delport?"

24

Cliffie Abrahams woke up feeling like a new man. Not one to dwell on the negative, the last few weeks were already a thing of the distant past. Like his stepdad Norm would have said, it wasn't about the cards life dealt you; it was how you played the hand. Leaving PE was the best thing he had done, because a fresh start was all that was needed to end the bad run of debt and outstanding warrants. He should have done it months ago.

A warm fuzziness coursing through his veins, Cliffie rolled out of bed, adjusted his morning glory, and strolled over to the window to greet the new day. Rhino Room was a total score, what with its own shower and toilet and view over the back garden. From behind the mesh curtain he surveyed the plunge pool – he would definitely be hitting it later with a couple of cold ones – Meissner's brak giving its balls a go, and the wifey at the washing line. As she reached over into the basket Cliffie caught a flash of white fleshy thigh; the bulge in his skants stiffened. It was time he took matters into his owns hands. With that, he headed for the shower.

Scrubbed and dressed in his Nashua sales rep outfit – black pants, white short-sleeve collared shirt, black shoes – Cliffie ambled into the dining room, where he encountered Otto Meissner waiting expectantly.

"Tops of the morning to you, Mr Abrahams! How did you sleep?"

"Like a baby, sir. Very comfortable beds you have here."

"We don't mess around."

"I can see that."

"I hope you have an appetite."

"That I do." In fact, Cliffie was ready to chew off the hind leg of a donkey.

Meissner drew an arc across the buffet table. "We have ... stewed fruits, corn flakes, guava juice, crackers and cheese, hardboiled eggs, Polony and ham slices, as much toast as you want, mixed fruit and apricot jam, all you can drink coffee and tea. Don't be shy, my friend."

"Nice. Very nice."

"Coffee now or later? … Excellent. Now and later."

Meissner headed into the kitchen, and Cliffie got to work on the buffet, stuffing his plate and mouth at equal pace. He sat down and assumed position, ready for battle. Meissner came in, set down the mug of coffee and pulled up a chair in front of him. He eyed Cliffie's loaded plate.

"So, my friend, what's the plan for the day?" Cliffie shovelled a spoonful of corn flakes into his mouth, buying extra seconds. He hadn't expected the guy to come out firing so early. "No rush, take your time." Meissner waited patiently while Cliffie chewed.

"Mind if I steal one of those paper tissues next to you?" Cliffie wiped his mouth, refolded the serviette. "The plan? Well, let me see … First, I must check if my Avis car is sorted, then I think I'll go to the bank to … to organise my finances. We've got some big package tours in the pipeline … with some big deposits that must come in, that type of thing." Cliffie popped a Salticrax into his mouth, thinking fast. "The American tourists pay top dollar for our Off the Beaten Track tours."

"Is that what you call them? Very interesting …"

"Like I was telling you last night, they're mad for this type of thing, especially the Americans. I must tell you, Otto, these prunes with the strawberry yoghurt are damn good." He stood up. "Time to move on to second course."

"Now that you mention it, I can actually see it."

"What?"

"Wealthy Americans arriving in Kombi buses. This area must be perfect for them, don't you think?"

"Oh, ja, it's huge business," said Cliffie, wandering back to the table with his plate overflowing with ham and cheese slices, the leftover boiled eggs, and a tower of white bread.

Meissner seized the gap. "It sounds like a good market for me to get into?"

Cliffie mopped an egg yellow with a corner of bread and popped it into his mouth. He sat back, chewing contemplatively. "A good market? It's more than a good market, Otto. Every time I think we've hit max, a call comes in for another tour. It's mad." He pulled out his cellphone – a Nokia 6210 with a crack down the middle of the screen. "Now that you remind me, I must check in quickly with HQ to find out where things are at."

"Go for it."

Cliffie strolled across to the bar with his mug of coffee. He dialled his own number, and held the phone to his ear, leaning up against the counter. Taking a sip, he gave Meissner a thumbs-up.

"Morning, Beverley! How things? … Ja, also all good my side. I've been made extremely comfortable … What's that? … Yes, top-drawer people. Unbelievable hospitality. Listen, Bev, I would love to chinwag all day, but is Victor in the office yet? … Well, please put me through." Clifford winked at Meissner. "You must meet this guy; a total nutcase. Sorry … Hey, Victor! How goes it? … Excellent, excellent… Listen, this line isn't so good. Can you tell me when my Avis car's arriving? … That's not what I want to hear, Victor … You tell them they better get their act together if they want our business … That's right, tomorrow morning by the latest. And another thing, where are we at with the down-payment from the Belgiums? Has it come through? … Vic, I don't care about promises; I care about money in the bank. And it's not like we're talking huge money. If they can't afford the two-bar, then they shouldn't be partnering with us … I'm going to the bank this morning, and I expect to see the cash … Okey-dokes, you let me know as soon as you hear something. I'll be back in the office by lunchtime tomorrow … Pub lunch at Squires Arms? Now we're talking, Vic. Anyways, we'll speak later. Ciao!"

Cliffie strolled back to the table. The guy hadn't budged – his ears were glowing pink. Like a juicy peach hanging from the tree, he was ripe for the picking.

"Sorry about that, Otto. Where were we, now?"

25

"You hit a cow or something, because this radiator's dead in its moer, pal."

The mechanic stood back from the Fortuner, enjoying his moment of schadenfreude.

"Can't you maybe weld it? Even if it's just temporary—"

"Do I look like Jesus and his loaves? Come, put your hand under here. You feel that Glenda Jackson crack? You lucky it didn't unpeel on you like a ripe banana. I won't even bother charging you for a welding stick."

"Have you then got stock of new radiators?"

"Plenty, pal."

Relief flooded Steve Aldridge's face; there was a God after all. "That's great. That's really great. For a moment I was worried—"

"Nissan bakkie? Plenty. Isuzu? Plenty. Tata? Plenty. Toyota Fortuner? Zilch. I have to order it."

"Are you serious, Mr Swanepoel? But how long will that take?"

The mechanic examined his hands. "What was it you said you hit again?"

"I didn't actually see it, but it must have been a buck."

Swanepoel rolled the clump of hair between his fingers. "This is no buck; way too soft … Too hard for a meercat or jackal … Feels more like bladdy human hair." He held the clump up to the light. "Maybe you're right, maybe you killed baby Bambi. And you didn't even stop to see if it was still alive? Hard core. Seriously hard core."

Aldridge squirmed under the mechanic's penetrating gaze. "I did try look for it, but—"

"My daughter will have you for breakfast if she hears this story. She doesn't even eat chicken; I'm talking mega bunny hugger." Swanepoel wiped his hands on his blue overalls. "If we order the thing today, it's minimum two days to get here, three hours to fit." He tapped his head. "That's if all goes to plan, touch wood. Which is never. You order a O-ring from these idiots? They send you a wedding ring. Then, if the agents get it right, the transport guys cock it up. Why? Because nobody in this country can tell their arses from their ears. My advice to you? Plan for three days, give or take a month on either side." Swanepoel flashed a jagged row of nicotine yellow at Aldridge. "Anyways, what's the rush? You're on holiday."

"But is there no way we can speed things up with a courier?"

"Speed things up? You think this is Joburg or Bloemfontein where you can get what you want by waving your magic wand. If you want to break down in the country, you must learn the ways of the country."

"I understand, but thought maybe—"

"This *is* with a transportation company, sir. What you take me for? Some interbreeding clown playing a banjo. If that's what you're thinking, maybe you must take your car elsewhere."

"Sorry, that's not what I meant, Mr Swanepoel. I appreciate everything you are doing, I really do. Please order the radiator, and I'll pay you the full amount now."

The mechanic softened his tone. "Not to worry, pal. I trust you, and you trust me. You pay me when the radiator arrives." He rolled his fingers. "You want my opinion? No ways in hell it was a buck you hit."

Back on the pavement outside Swanie's Diesel Repairs, Aldridge squinted into the North West glare. Beads of cold sweat trickled down his back. First the open caravan door, now this – it was too close for comfort. What if there was more hair stuck in the grill? What if the guy opened his big mouth to other customers? What if …

Bordered by industrial palisade on one side, burnt veld on the other, the street felt eerie and deserted. Across the road, a crossbreed Alsatian-something on a tight chain eyed him from behind the fence. Aldridge glanced back uneasily. Swanepoel was now standing at the workshop window, talking to someone on the phone. This was most definitely not going according to Tarryn's grand plan.

Weaving around the potholes, Aldridge quickened the pace.

Three days for the radiator to arrive, maybe longer – there was no ways he would survive three more days of this. His mind was racing, grabbing at straws. There had to be another option. Like, they could hire an Avis car from Pretoria or some other town – an Avis car with a big boot – then drive into the middle of nowhere, take care of business, and only come back when the car was fixed. Yes, they would have to transfer *him* from the caravan to the boot, but they would do it late at night and make sure nobody saw them. It was risky and terrifying as all hell, but not half as risky and terrifying compared to doing nothing.

Aldridge rounded the corner into unfamiliar territory.

Again, he could feel them – the eyes, watching him from behind dark windows. Hurrying on, he stayed close to the shadows of the giant blue gum trees growing out the tar. Up ahead, a green plastic banner hung loosely above the road.

EDENDAL AGRI FEES. 24 OCTOBER.
ALL WELKOM! ANNUAL POTJIE SHOWDOWNE!
FOOD STALLS GALORE! MISS EDEN!
SAPS DEMO!! MUSIC! BEER TENT! AND LOTS MORE!

To the front he caught a glimpse of the church steeple piercing the rooftops; it meant the guesthouse had to be close by. A horse on the home trot, Aldridge broke into a shuffling jog. He hadn't run for ages, but that was all going to change when he got home and joined Planet Fitness. He would sign up for their life membership, because that's how committed he was. Breathing hard, he slowed the pace; Rockies sandals weren't the best to run in.

He was now back in familiar territory. He recognised the cafe on the left, and the four-way stop where that mangy dog had blocked the road. If he remembered right, the Eden sign was just a bit further on. He suddenly felt hungry, like he could eat one of those thick sirloin steaks dripping in cheese-and-mushroom sauce that they served back home at the Black Jackal. In fact, that's what he would do – take Tarryn out for a meal on the town. His treat. It would do her good. Help her relax before he unveiled his Plan B.

Up ahead, Eden's razor wire shimmered under the hot haze. The Jurgens looked lonely and forlorn under the blue gum trees. The knot in his gut tightened. It was pushing it, but if they got their act together and ordered a car from Avis Nelspruit, they could be on the road before midnight; it wasn't impossible. Because, like that American guy said, IMPOSSIBLE was just another word for I'M-POSSIBLE. Tarryn could make some excuse about her mom landing in hospital. She was better with these things than— Aldridge came to a frozen halt.

Otto Meissner's dog had appeared from behind the caravan. His head was held up high, sniffing the air. His eyes had a look of intense concentration. The knot in Aldridge's gut ratcheted up several notches as the object of concentration came into mental view: the caravan itself. More specifically, something *inside* the caravan. To Aldridge's fast mounting horror, Adolf reared up and pressed his muzzle into the door. There was no mistaking it: the stalactite of drool glistening in the late morning sun.

26

Ferdie Meyer placed his hand over the mouthpiece and waved the sales rep to the Addis chair opposite.

"Be with you in a sec, buddy."

"No worries."

"Like I said, Waynie, things this side are tighter than a nun's twat; my customers can't afford that type of money. That's why I say, send me the five Dreamliners on consignment and we see how it goes. If they sell, I pay you cash and order another ten on the spot. If they don't, you take them back ... Ja, Standard Series is perfecto; nobody here's gonna buy the Executive." Meyer replaced the phone. "I tell you."

"Problem?"

"Just another day in Africa. These fat cat importers sitting behind their desks in Joburg are clueless about business in the platteland. So, anyways, what can I do you for?"

The rep handed his business card across the desk. "Johnny Angel. Global Clean."

Meyer studied it. *"It doesn't have to cost the earth.* I like that. You some sort of cleaning products agent?

"Much bigger than that. Think of us as your first link in the wholesale chemical supply chain."

"Where you based?"

"Head office, Durban, branches across Africa. You name it, no matter what the industry, Global's there."

"Like what exactly?"

The rep looked up at the ceiling. "Jissus, where do I start? Abattoirs are a big one. Hospitals, another biggie. Food factories, municipalities, old-age homes, and so on. That's for our general cleaners, your Handy Andys and

Jeyes Fluids, but I'm talking industrial scale – chemical super tanker scale. This is another biggie, especially in Nigeria." He steered the photocopied catalogue across the desk. "Those are just some of the turnkey solutions we make for you guys."

Angel watched Meyer flip through the catalogue.

"Take our Supergrade Ammonia Solvent at the top there. It was first designed for abattoirs, for the grease traps, but since this virus thing, it's one of our best sellers with mortuaries and hospitals. Unbelievable stuff; cuts through fat and grease like a knife through butter."

"And costs a fat whack, I bet."

"That's what people think. But because we import in bulk we can pass on the discount to the customer."

"Now you're talking my language."

"Also don't forget our product is super concentrated, not like the local junk. Same when you buy dishwasher liquid. Do you go for the Sunlight for twenty-three bucks or the no-name brand for fifteen?"

The rep had touched a raw spot. Meyer had been stung by this one, or rather, his wife had. The woman hadn't let go until that poor manager at the Check-In swapped the open box of Supa-Brite for the OMO. He pulled at his ear.

"Even so, price still comes into it. You heard me on the phone, us small guys can't afford these fancy imported products."

"I hear you, but tell you what. How about you give me

a walk-through your place, and I'll give you a free needs analysis?"

Meyer hesitated. He had Henley and Glen Mitchell to sort out. On the other hand, he was looking for any excuse to tell those bullshitting sleazebags from Zenith Industrial Solutions to go to hell. He was still convinced they were diluting the embalming fluid. "What the hell, let's do it; I'll give you the grand tour." He pushed his chair back. "One other thing. Do your prices include VAT?"

"VAT. Free delivery. Sixty-day payment terms,"

That sealed it for Meyer. Zenith could go to hell.

Meyer led the way into the showroom, past a row of coffins standing like sentries against the wall. He stroked the high-gloss finish. "Is this a beaut, or what? More specs than a Ferrari. Solid wood, triple-layer buttoned velvet, brass handles, the works. Bet you won't believe I paid less than three grand each for these before the rand went down the toilet. I should have bought fifty."

"Why so cheap?"

"Simple. Last year's fashions aren't good enough for the Americans. So, what happens? The manufacturers are left with a warehouse of V-4s. So, what do they do? They ship them to us Third World countries." Meyer gave the rep a moment to ponder this absurdity of modern consumerism, before pulling back the curtain and unlocking the fire door leading to the mortuary. "You ready?"

"For sure."

The mortuary was a converted walk-in fridge — a throwback to the early '80s, when New Horizons served life as a butchery. A heap of charred corpses was stacked high in the corner. The centre of the room was taken up by two stainless steel trolleys draped in dirty sheets, from which two pairs of hairy feet protruded, each with a tightly-wound tag attached to a big toe. Meyer indicated to the tangled mess in the corner.

"We're still sorting through that one," he said, apologetically. "Taxi head-on."

"No worries, friend. I saw worse in Angola."

Meyer lifted a sheet. "In that case, check this one that just came in. The wife found him still staring at the TV when she got back from her bowls."

The rep flipped the toe tag over: "Glen Mitchell. What happened?"

"Still waiting for the DS report, but I reckon asthma attack." Meyer dropped the sheet. "Same with old Roger Henley here."

The rep stepped in for a closer look. "Why they both so blue?"

"That's nothing, pal. You should have seen them before we did our thing. Purple in the face and neck like I've never seen before."

"Also asthma attack?"

"Could be. But that would be weird."

"What would be?"

"If both of them pegged from asthma aanvals on the exact same day." Meyer flicked open the brown folder lying on the table alongside. "At least their families won't be going hungry."

"What you mean?"

"Fat life policies, both of them. Talk about hitting the Lotto …"

"Why so?"

"Why so? Because Henley here only signed up on 4 May this year."

"And the other one?"

Meyer bent over Mitchell's file. "Ka-ching! Three Feb! The brokers must be laughing all the way to the bank." Meyer tossed the folder to the side and anxiously eyed the wall clock above the fridges. "Don't want to rush you, but I've got a funeral to organise. You want to sell me some cleaning chemicals, or not?"

27

"Don't be a wuss, man – get in there with them. My babies don't bite."

Botes glanced nervously behind him, averting the eyes of the agitated white lioness pacing up and down the game fence. Lions had never been his thing, and Jakkals knew it.

"Ag, don't worry about her. She's just an overgrown

kitten."

"You sure the electricity is switched on? I swear that thing looks like she wants to jump the fence, Jakkie."

Jakkals Venter cackled. "Nooit going to happen. Unless she wants fifty thousand volts to go through her poepol." He was enjoying the moment. "Here, grab my mug. I'll fetch one for you to hold."

"Seriously, I don't need to. Mustn't we just leave them alone, before the mother gets even more pissed off?"

Jakkals stepped into the pen and waded into his pride and joy. "All right, all right, don't get all excited now. Connie, check how happy they are to see me. It's like they think I'm their mom. Hey, get off my leg! The claws on these little shits can slice you open like razor wire. I said, off!" Jakkals slapped the cub across the head. It released its grip and rolled across the sawdust, yelping.

"Jesus, Jakkie, that was a stywe klap," laughed Botes, checking anxiously behind him that the cub's mother was still behind the fence.

"You have to show them who is boss; it's the law of the jungle, Connie. This little bliksem's not even six months and he wants to take me out. Amazing, hey? Not like us pathetic humans." Jakkals grabbed hold of another cub and lifted it into the air, squirming and hissing. "Check this power." Without warning, he reached over the pen and thrust the cub into Botes's unwilling arms. "Whatever you do, don't drop him. The bitch mother will go befok if you do."

Botes staggered back under the weight and writhing power of the cub, which was hissing in his face like a cornered Cape cobra. "Jesus, Jakkie, I can hardly hold onto him. Eina! The thing scratched me!"

"That's because you're hugging him to death," laughed Jakkals. "Keep it away from you so he can't reach with its claws."

Botes was starting to panic. And so was the cub in his grip. Below, the earth rumbled with a bloodcurdling growl that cut straight to Botes' primal fear centre. "Please, Jakkie, I can't hold him any more. You take him. Shit, I'm gonna drop him!" The cub hit the ground with a heavy thud. Jakkals had stopped laughing. His eyes had turned icy.

"You fucking mad, or what? You want to kill him?"

"Sorry, man, I couldn't hold him any more." Botes lifted two bleeding arms in his defence.

"I don't care a fuck, Connie. You don't drop it from a height and tell me it's fine. What if it broke a leg? You know what these things are worth?"

"I said I'm sorry, Jakkals."

"Come on, tell me. Five grand? Ten grand?"

"I don't know."

"In that case, let me tell you what a fat American hunter will pay for a juvenile white lion. Twenty thousand US dollars, Conrad!" He spat out the words. "Multiply by thirteen. What's that give you?"

Still in shock, Botes crunched through the maths. "Two

hundred and sixty?"

"Exactly. Multiply again by kak exchange rate. We're talking white gold here, boytjie."

"I'm sorry, man. I thought you were keeping them as pets or something."

Jakkals Venter slapped his comrade's shoulder. "Pets? That's a good one. Like old Jakkals needs a pack of white lions for pets. Come, let's enjoy our dop under the lapa and talk business."

Botes trailed his boss to the thatch lapa and the remains of a bottle of Scotch and two glasses set out on a tray.

"I want you to tell me what you think of this Glenfiddich; my daughter bought it for my birthday. Cost her a whack." Jakkals poured. "Salute! To the future and all that."

"Very nice. Very smooth."

"Very nice. Very smooth," echoed Jakkals in his best Queen's English. "Don't give me that stront. Why don't you just be honest and say it tastes like charcoal?"

"No, seriously, it tastes different to the usual—"

"Blah, blah. No wonder I can't ever get straight answers out of you lot."

"No, really, Jakkie—"

"Relax, man, I'm pulling your chain. Of course it's good stuff. You think I would give you horse piss?" Jakkals reached for the bottle and topped up his glass. "Enough funny games. How did it go with that last one?"

"All good, hey. No problems to report."

Jakkals Venter gave his crotch a scratch. "Good to hear.

You heard about the thing with Dippies?"

"Ja, Freddie told me. There must be a logical explanation."

"We can't afford mistakes, Connie."

"No mistakes my side, Jakkals," said Botes, dabbing at the deep scratch on his arm with his hanky.

"You sure about that?"

"Hundred per cent. That latest batch we got from the agent is working like a dream. You can ask Dippies. We're talking two minutes flat from start to finish."

"Well, just make sure it carries on working like a dream. What about the side effects?"

"What side effects?"

"I don't know, what if the guy's on heavy antibiotics or something? What happens then? What if the two don't mix and it stays in the system?"

"Co-variable studies have shown no significant change in detection levels—"

"Plain and simple English, please, Professor."

"It will make no difference, Jakkie. This stuff is top-drawer. The Russians have spent years perfecting it."

Venter gave his crotch a dig. "This stuff's too high tech for my boer brain. But as long as it's working like you say it's working, then I'm happy."

"Like a dream, Jakkie. I'm telling you, it's the way of the future."

"In that case, maybe we must start replacing some of our old methods with the new. Keep up with the times, and all that. This latest incident with Dippies is making me jumpy as a cricket."

"You're hundred per cent right, Jakkie. If we want to stay in the game, we have to go high tech. You won't believe the pharmaceutical developments that are happening nowadays. American B-52 bombers have nothing on the new chemical cocktails coming out—"

Jakkals's phone was vibrating on the lapa's bar counter.

"The old duiwel himself. He better have good news for me … Freddie Ferreira! What you got?"

While Jakkals paced around the pool, giving Freddie an earful and scratching his crotch at the same time, Conrad Botes dipped the corner of his hanky into his whisky and dabbed gingerly at his wounds.

28

Hearing the crunch of approaching footsteps, Tarryn Aldridge parted the blind and peered through. Steve. She pulled the slider on the lock and opened the caravan door a crack.

"What the heck took you so long?" she whispered.

Aldridge hurriedly passed the bags of ice through to her. "You don't know what it's like out there; I had to go to three different places after they started giving me funny looks at the garage."

"How many did you get?"

"Six."

"Is that all?"

"Must I get more? I will if you want."

"Don't worry, I'll see how it goes. Did you get the pruning shears?"

"Under the ice. It was the last pair left at the Agri. This is crazy—"

"And the black bags?"

"They're together with the pruners. What must I do now?"

"Like we discussed, Steve, act as if you're fixing something on the caravan. Whatever you do, don't forget to bang on the side if someone comes. We're dead if you don't."

"I can't believe we're doing this, Tarryn. It's not moral."

Tarryn eyed her husband through the gap. His face was paler than the time he caught tick bite fever at Hartebeespoort. "Yes, yes, you've already told me. How do you think I feel? I'm the one who has to do the job, not you. Anyway, we don't have time any more for your grand Plan B. Did you get the car fixed? No! Did you find a car to hire? No! After the break-in last night and that horrible dog sniffing around, do we have a choice? No! We have to do what we have to do, Steve. And I'll do it, with or without you."

"I'm just saying—"

"Enough just saying." With that, Tarryn shut the caravan door in his face and locked it.

It was forever and a day ago since she had last helped with a slaughter. Twenty years, maybe more — the last time must have been during the school holidays when she was in matric. But like riding a bike, it was something you never forgot. Especially the first time: a dry berg wind day before her tenth birthday, just a few weeks after her dad landed the farm manager job outside Estcourt. She could still see herself, perched on that empty oil drum, watching the whole thing from beginning to end, like it was some Disney movie. Then afterwards helping the maids in the kitchen cut up the meat and wrap it in Jiffy for the deep freeze, while her brother Jason stayed hidden under his bed.

After that first time she quickly lost track of all the cattle dragged in and killed on the concrete slab behind the workshop.

Tarryn took quick stock of her work space. It was just as well Steve had decided in the end to splurge on the 601, because the Jurgens Junior would have been a nightmare to work in. It didn't even come with a foldaway table.

She reached into the stowaway above the bunk bed and brought out the camping tablecloth. The thick plastic would be perfect for the job. She spread it open on the Formica table, and moved the bunk seat cushions out of harm's way.

Next, she slid open the cutlery drawer and selected her tools. The Samurai Chef Set from Verimark was a definite. For back-up, she added a paring and deboning knife and two steak knives, which she arranged in a neat row next to the tools Steve had bought. As an afterthought, she reached back into the drawer for the bread knife – one never knew what to expect.

It was way too big for her, but Steve's Braai-Meester apron would have to do. To mop up any other mess, she added a three-pack dishcloth set, a roll of Carlton paper towel, and several black garbage bags to the prep table. She emptied most of the five-litre bottle of La Vie into the plastic basin and gave it a squirt of Sunlight. Her hands were shaking from the adrenalin, but not so badly that she couldn't control them. Her dad would have actually been proud of her if he was still alive.

A female UFC cage fighter about to enter the ring, Tarryn sucked in a deep breath; it was now or never. Peeling away the duvet cover, she pulled *him* to the middle of the Formica table – he was stiffer than an ironing board. She hadn't even started and the stare was already making her uncomfortable. She reached for one of the dish cloths and dropped it over the face. Problem sorted.

Biting into her lip, she quickly cut away the jogging shorts and the vest. Without the clothes he looked more skinned rabbit than human. Compared to a cow or sheep, there was hardly anything to him – which would make her job much easier. With the veggie cutting board wedged under his back, his bony chest protruded outwards and his arms pulled nicely to the back.

Opting for the Samurai General Utility, Tarryn began with a Y-shape cut: from the skinny shoulders to the lower end of the chest bone. It was like cutting through bread, and the Samurai performed just like they advertised on TV. She could well believe it, the blade *could* probably cut through a block of wood.

Using one of the serrated steak knives, she sliced downwards towards the pubic bone, taking a wide detour around the belly button just like her dad had taught her. To her surprise, there wasn't much blood at all. She wiped the sweat from her forehead – even with the roof vent open the caravan was like an oven – and lifted the blind. Steve was tapping anxiously at the spare wheel with a spanner. Good. She checked her watch; twenty minutes had flown by. She needed to get a move on.

Taking the pliers, she proceeded to pull away the skin and muscle. A strong whiff of raw lamb filled the caravan. Her wrist and forearm ached. Stopping for a quick breather, she sized up the cheapo pruners Steve had bought from the Agri. They definitely didn't look up for the job, but beggars couldn't be choosers. Her wrist still burning, Tarryn pushed on. It was getting to be hard work – like carving a Sunday roast with a bread knife – and she was heaving and grunting under the effort as she cut away at the flesh. But eventually she had the rib cage open. She lifted it off.

Several neat slashes later with the Samurai paring knife, the organs were free. Taking great care not to mess, she lifted these out and dropped them into the waiting black bag that was lined with ice. She should have told Steve to buy at least eight bags, because if the weather stayed hot like this, they would have to keep topping up. But she would cross that bridge when she got to it, because right now she had to concentrate on the arms and legs.

Fifteen minutes later Tarryn was just about done and the pruners were still holding out. She had kept the worst job for last – her dad had fired a worker on the spot for messing it up – but there was no stopping her now. Leaning over the remains – not that there had been much to start with in the first place – she cut away the intestines. Taking extra special care, she slid them slowly across the tablecloth, off the edge of the table, and into the plastic bucket. The stench hit her head-on; she'd totally forgotten how bad it could be.

Tarryn had lost track of time. In fact, it felt like she had done the entire operation in one of those Indian religion trances. Her body was suddenly feeling it though – her back, her shoulders, her wrists, even her calves ached. She did a final sweep of the caravan. The table was wiped clean. The tools were washed and packed away. The recycling bags were knotted and stacked neatly in the locked wardrobe. The two Colemans were hidden under the table. There was enough ice to keep things fresh for another day. Two black bags – one with rubbish, the other with offal – stood ready to go at the door. She had used a full roll of Carlton and all the dishcloths. It was a real pity she had to get rid of the Braai-Meester apron she'd given Steve for his birthday. It was a nice one, from Outdoor Warehouse in Bedfordview.

29

Like a bloated tick on a sheep's arse, the thing with Freddie and Dippenaar had lodged itself in Truter's brain and was refusing to let go. He needed relief, and he needed it fast.

"Delport!"

A moment later his deputy's shadow hovered outside the office door. "You called, sir?"

"Ja, there's something important I want to discuss with you. Don't be shy, man, come in and take a seat." Truter pushed the Chicken-Licken takeaway to the side, then scraped off a blob of Wing Commander sauce from his trouser crotch, and licked his fingers. "Go for it, there's still some slap chips left in the box."

Delport shifted uneasily in the chair. "I'm fine, sir."

Delport was lucky to have caught him in a generous mood, but if that's how he wanted to play it … "How are my stats for Pretoria coming on?"

"Actually, quite well, sir."

"What earthmoving discoveries have you made?"

"Nothing like that, but I am finding the process quite interesting."

Truter contemplated the earnest freckly face sitting across the desk. The guy would be so lost without him. "I'm glad to hear you find it interesting. That is why I assigned you with the job. You do know that?"

"Yes, sir. And I appreciate it."

"But since we're talking valuable taxpayer's money, what exactly have you found so far?" Truter rummaged in his takeaway bag for the wet wipe. "Carry on, I'm listening."

"Umm … it's a bit early to say but I am starting to see some patterns—"

"Like what? I need specifics."

"Well, one thing I've picked up so far is the high number of pedestrian deaths we've had in the North West over the past quarter."

"Quarter what?"

"Sorry, three months. For some reason, the stats have spiked compared to last year. If it carries on like this to the end of—"

"Fascinating." Truter wiped his mouth, rolled the wet wipe into a ball, and pitched it at the bin in the corner. "Cowabunga! How's that for a hole in one, Delport! Am I good, or what?"

"Very nice one, sir … The figures are almost five times higher for the period in question. But that's only for white males."

"'The period in question.' Where the hell do you come with these fancy words, I ask."

Delport pushed on bravely. "That was the first

interesting thing I noticed. The other is Domestic Deaths by Natural Causes. The figures are also much higher for the past three months, but again it's only for white males. Which is strange if you stop and think about—"

"Thank you, I get the picture, Constable Sherlock Holmes, and I'm sure our colleagues in Pretoria are going to be very impressed with your work." The tick in Truter's head had started burrowing again. It was time to cut through the foreplay. "Delport, what can you tell me about the insurance business?"

"You mean like life insurance?"

"Ja, life insurance, funeral insurance, that type of jazz. What do you know about it?"

"Apart from my own policy and what my sister Glenda told me, I can't really say I know too much."

"You never told me you had a sister? Jirre, I hope she didn't inherit your genes, because that would now be an environmental disaster."

"Glenda's actually my half-sister."

"See, I told you there's a God, Delport. Anyways, what's your sister got to do with insurance?"

"She's an actuary with Santam."

Truter rolled his eyes. "Here we go again. What the hell's an actually?"

"An actuary. They're involved with the mathematics behind the insurance business, which is used to work out the odds of certain insurance events happening."

"So, what you're saying is she's a fortune teller who can

predict earthquakes? Or when someone will peg off?"

"Not exactly, sir, but they can work out general patterns by analysing the stats of thousands of people. From this they calculate the insurance premiums they must charge. If I remember right, Glenda called it mathematical risk modelling."

"More like mathematical hocus pocus."

"It makes sense if you think about it, sir. For example, even we know that guys in their twenties have more car accidents than guys in their fifties. That's why car insurance premiums are higher for younger guys."

Truter was impressed. "Maybe so, but predicting tsunamis and all, that's a load of horse kak." He stretched across the desk and scratched in the takeaway box for the remains of bread roll. "I have another question for you. What can you tell me about funeral insurance companies?"

"Again, only what I know from having my own policy. Most of the time it's the same company who sells life insurance and funeral—"

"Because you won't believe the stories Ferdie Meyer's been telling me about people leaving their families in the dwang because they've gone with some fly-by-night." Truter chewed contemplatively. "I bet you don't know how much a decent white man's funeral costs nowadays? We're talking thousands, Delport. I mean, like tens of thousands."

"That is true. Funerals are very expensive."

"How are you going to afford that on your SAPS

salary?"

"That's why I have taken out a funeral policy, sir. What's great about the company I'm with is they offer free funeral cover when you take out life cover with them."

"Is that a fact?"

"And they've got this loyalty club, where you can earn bonus points and prizes."

"Prizes? What prizes?"

"All sorts. Spur vouchers, cellphones, mags for your car, expensive pots and pans, you name it, sir. You can even win holidays to Sun City."

"Sounds too good to be true, Delport." Truter pushed back on his chair. This was going nowhere fast. "Okay, Delport, I think we're done. Thank you for your time."

Delport stood up hurriedly. "Pleasure, sir. I'm glad I could be of assistance."

"And close the door behind you."

Truter waited until Delport was out of earshot, picked up the phone and dialled the number. Meyer answered on the second ring.

"New Horizons at your service."

"Ferdie, it's Truter."

"Hey, Trutes, what's up, pal?"

"Not so much, but can I ask you something quick?"

"Okay, but it better be snappy. I've got Mitchell's old lady about to walk in for a viewing."

"You remember yesterday?"

"Ja, it was the day before today."

"I mean, you remember showing me that yellow form from one of the companies you deal with?"

"The policy form. What about it?"

"Can you remember what the name was?"

"The company's name?"

"Ja."

"TFS. AKA Titanium Financial Services."

"That's the one. Will you check something else for me on the form?"

"Jissus, Trutes, what's this about?

"Please, man."

"Okay, fokkit, hang on a sec, I'll have to pull it out."

Truter waited. His tongue felt thick in his mouth.

"Got it. What's it you want to know?"

"If you look at the bottom of the page, I think there was some people's names typed there?"

"Okay, it says here: 'Directors: JD Venter. F Ferreira. CE Botes.' Is that what you mean? ... You still there?"

"Ja, I'm here. Thanks. That's all I wanted to know."

"Good. Can I go now? The woman's coming up the driveway."

Truter set the phone down slowly. He leant forwards, elbows on the desk, hands behind his head, finger massaging his old shrapnel scar. He stared into the chipped wood veneer, trying to untangle his scrambled thoughts. The bloated tick had just burrowed itself deeper into his brain.

30

Tarryn rubbed the tennis ball between her husband's shoulders; smaller bulges marked a knotty trail up his neck. For better or worse, through sickness and in health, until death do us part. That's what they had promised each other.

Edendal lay behind them. The future stretched out ahead, along a corrugated dirt road cutting between two mielie fields.

"Going for this walk was a good idea."

"I know. I was starting to go loopy in the room, staring at that stupid black-and-white TV."

"This whole thing's crazy, Tarryn."

"It is. But I'm feeling a bit calmer now. Aren't you?"

"Guess so. I'm telling you, the second the car's fixed, we are out of here big time. They won't even sniff our dust."

"I can't wait. Just the idea of hitching the caravan and driving off into the sunset gives me a serious case of the goosebumps."

"Tell me about it. What you say we make up for lost time and push on straight for Kruger and try have a nice holiday?"

"I would definitely drink to that."

"And don't forget I managed to score one of those riverfront stands at Satara. It would be a pity to waste it because of a ... temporary detour."

Tarryn squeezed her husband's hand. "Temporary detour. That's a funny way to describe it."

"Glad you think so," said Aldridge, returning the squeeze.

They walked on for a while, neither saying anything, content in each other's company.

"It's actually quite pretty out here," said Tarryn.

"Maybe the town isn't as bad as we've been making it out to be. It just seems that way because of this thing." Aldridge tapped the side of his head with his free hand. "It's all in here, babes."

"What is?"

"Reality. It's what you make of it. Scientific studies have proved that humans can programme their brain to be anything they want it to be. If you can think it, you can be it!"

"Amazing."

"We did this exercise on the Dale Carnegie course where you focus on a negative thought and turn it into a positive one. And I promise you, it works. Our instructor said that was the main difference between people who survived the concentration camps and those who didn't."

"It's great to hear you speak so positive like this." A paramedic giving CPR to a road accident victim, Tarryn pumped her husband's hand with renewed urgency. "All along I knew you had it in you."

"So, let's try it …" Aldridge drew an arc with his free hand across the skyline. "In your mind, picture the sun dropping behind the camel thorn trees as we arrive at Satara, and that sweet smell of the African bush after the rain ..."

"Carry on, I'm starting to like this."

"Okay ... Now imagine us setting up camp on the green grass overlooking the river ... The elephants at the waterhole with their babies ..."

"Sounds amazing. I can actually see it."

"Keep your eyes shut ... We've just started the fire and are settling down in our camping chairs, you with your glass of white wine and those Salticrax with chive cream cheese, me with my Windhoek Draught that's all frosty on the outside from being in the Engel so long."

"Now you're really torturing me. I wish we could hit Fast Forward and be there this very second."

Aldridge gently extricated himself from his wife's grip. "If you can hold that picture in your mind until this is over, you *can* go there whenever you want to."

"You're so wise."

"It's all about Attitude. Spelt with a capital A, by the way."

"I was about to say the same thing."

They had reached the tar road. A T-junction. A crossroads with a choice attached: continue on or return. The mood downshifted a gear.

"That must be the road we'll be driving out on."

Fending off a knife stab of longing, Tarryn stared into the hazy horizon. No matter what new curve balls came their way, she was determined to hold on to this feeling of freedom. "I suppose we better get back."

Steve and Tarryn Aldridge turned and started walking slowly back in the direction of Edendal. To the west, a pall of grey hung heavy over the township.

"I wonder what Mike and the guys are getting up to."

"No good, I bet."

"Apparently they were planning a boys' fishing trip to Allemansdrift. Gary's bought himself a new six-sleeper that he wants to test out."

"Can you just imagine?"

"Ja, I bet they're hitting the ales this very second."

"And talking a load of nonsense."

"That's no lie. Mike should have been a stand-up, the way he carries on. You must hear him at work; he has Mr Edwards down to a tee."

"That can't be so hard. What do they call that shaking disease, anyway?"

"You're thinking of Parkinson's. But it's not that. The lopsided thing with his mouth is because of a stroke he had a few years ago, but his brain is still razor-sharp. You won't believe it, Edwards is the only guy at work who doesn't have to check the catalogue for the bearing codes."

"Is that a hawk on the telephone pole?"

"Looks more like a kestrel … I bet they're having a fat party … I'll never forget that time at Shelley Point when Mike hid a pilchard in Sean's fishing boot? That was so classic."

"You said something about Sean only discovering it much later?"

"Ja, like only the next morning later."

"Okay, tell me. I know you're dying to."

"So … here we are fishing at the pier for more than an hour already when Sean sniffs the air and says all innocent-like, 'What's that smell?' I swear, Gary almost fell into the water, he was in such stitches."

"That's funny. Especially the way you describe it."

"But that's not the end of the story … An hour later we're heading back to Seabreeze all hot and sweaty, and Sean plonks himself down in front of the caravan and tells Michelle to bring him a beer. I swear, it was like watching a Hollywood movie in slow motion, what with Michelle walking towards Sean with a cold one and about to hand it to him when Sean decides now's a good time to kick off his boots. Whack! The stench hits them both head-on. I'm not exaggerating, vrot pilchard is smeared everywhere. Between his toes, around his ankle, all the way down his foot." Aldridge wiped the tears away. "Oh hell, it feels so good to laugh again."

"That is *so* disgusting."

"You telling me; I almost puked. I'll never forget that moment for as long as I live."

"It was probably the cause of them getting divorced."

"I never thought of it like that."

"I was only kidding."

"I know, but I still feel bad for both of them, even

though it was Sean's fault for messing up."

Eden Palm had come into view.

"What's wrong, babes?"

Tarryn turned away and roughly brushed at the tears that had come from nowhere. "It's nothing, I'm fine." She sucked in deeply, held the air, exhaled slowly. "I don't know how much longer I can take this, Stevie. I swear I'm going to crack if we don't get out of here soon. Today, in the caravan ... I can't get *him* out of my head."

Steve Aldridge pulled his wife to him and held her tight, pressing her head into his chest. "We are going to get out of here. I promise you, T, no matter what it takes, I am going to get us out of here."

Tarryn lifted her face to his. "I know you will. I'm sorry, I don't know what happened there; it came out of the blue. I really want to be strong for you."

"And I want to be strong for you."

They kissed long and slow against the blood-red horizon.

"I love you."

"I love you, too."

"I love you more than all the galaxies of stars in the sky."

"I love you more than all the grains of sand on all the beaches in the—"

"Stevie, what's that over there?"

"Where?"

"There ... In front of the gate."

Aldridge turned and followed Tarryn's gaze. "No ways, it can't be!"

But it was. A police van parked in front of Eden Palm B&B. With an all-too familiar bull of a human in a blue SAPS uniform leaning casually up against it.

31

Otto Meissner planted a wet kiss on the dog's head.

"What's up with you, Dolfie, my boy? Suddenly not eating a thing, moping about like you're not interested in life." He clambered back to his feet and hiked his khaki shorts. "Sergeant, you've seen what Adolf is usually like. Always so full of beans."

Truter grunted; his lead-lined riot boot knew all too well what Adolf was usually like. "You checked him for the biliary?"

Worry flashed over Meissner's face. "You think that is it?"

"For sure. When I was with Benoni Dog Unit and we had a Rottie that wasn't lus for the kill, we just put him on the tabs, and he'd be right as rain."

"That must be it then. And here I was thinking he is bored with his diet." Meissner fought back the lump in his throat. "He's a very sensitive animal, as you know."

Truter squinted into the setting sun, at the couple

emerging slowly through it. "We've got company."

"Don't worry, that's just my guests from Vanderbijl. Jumpy as sparrows, both of them … Mr and Mrs Odridge!" Meissner shouted across the way. A menacing growl floated up from below. The couple approached cautiously. "Come now, don't be scared, my dog won't bite … See what I mean?" he whispered over his shoulder. "So, my friends, how was your walk?"

"It was nice, thank you," said the woman.

Truter had seen these two somewhere before. He shifted his bulk to face them head-on, blocking the path.

"How can one not enjoy our beautiful town? Don't you agree, Sergeant?"

"Hundreds. It's a sin against the creator if you don't appreciate every day." Truter locked onto a faint outline of nipple.

"Wise words," said Meissner. "Not only is our police chief a crime-fighting machine, he's also a spiritual man. And, and, if you don't mind me mentioning, Sergeant, a braai master of note … Don't try deny it, now. It was you, my friend, who taught those clowns from Southern Districts the true meaning of potjie last year."

"That is but true." Truter had definitely seen these two characters somewhere before.

Meissner furled back his lip and flashed a row of yellow at the couple – one-part sarcastic grin, one-part snigger. "I don't know if it's true, but there's a rumour going around that these city-slickers are planning to give us locals a hiding at tomorrow's Showdown."

"Is that now a fact?" said Truter, his jaw tightening. His eyes shifted to the black bra strap peeping through the neck of the T-shirt.

"Unfortunately, it looks like we have to leave first thing in the morning—"

"Nonsense, Mrs Odridge. My wife has gone to a lot of trouble to organise you people an entry ticket."

Mrs Odridge turned to her husband. "What do you think, Steve? Will the … hospital let us visit outside visiting hours?"

"I'm … I'm not sure."

She turned back to Meissner. "We got a call earlier that Steve's mother has had … a stroke. We need to get back as soon as—"

"As soon as we've treated you to true country hospitality. Not so, Sergeant?"

Truter grunted in agreement. A synapse had fired in his head. Odridge? How come he knew the name? Was it from the TV? These two didn't fit the typical Crime Watch profile, but that meant squat. The Snowdown character was a case in point – he also didn't look like a terrorist, but meanwhile, back at the ranch … Truter could feel the sweat coming off these two. He could smell it. He could just about taste it.

"Sorry, Sergeant, I see we're taking up your valuable time here. Before we were interrupted you were saying about my employee disappearing and now there's a missing person's case on him?"

"Yebo! Last time his chick-wife saw him was sparrow's fart two days ago. According to her, he went for his jog and vanished into space. Didn't come home, didn't call on the phone, didn't send a SMS. Next thing, she hits the panic button and opens a missing person's."

"Incredible."

Not one to waste a captive audience, Truter continued: "And next thing after that, we've escalated to a high-profile priority status case. Pretoria HQ, Special Investigations, Potch CID, you name it, I've got them all working twenty-four seven on it."

"Are you serious, Sergeant?"

"Big-time serious. Faxes and intermails coming at us non-stop, my own staff working overtime." Without warning, Truter pulled up the handbrake. "This is highly confidential stuff, so don't even think of blabbing your mouths off." His tone was laced with menace, far from the earlier pellie-pellie. His eyes had also glazed over, as something clicked in his brain. Aldridge! He had finally remembered. He turned to the city slapgat, whose skin was looking whiter than a jockstrap soaked overnight in OMO. What did a chick like her see in him? The guy couldn't even stand up straight.

"Meneer, are you SJ Aldridge?"

"Yes … why do you ask?"

"I've got a present for you." Truter reached into the van's window and retrieved the K-Way jacket. "Catch!"

The confused look on slapgat's face reminded Truter of a springhare caught in his headlights, just before he clipped it.

"Where did you find it?"

"This isn't the old South Africa, meneer. You must look after your things."

"Ja, I'm also confused," said Meissner. "Where did you find it?"

Truter chuckled. "You'll like this one, Meissner." He leant back against the van, taking his time. "My professional colleague arrives at the station this morning and trips over this vuil dronkie lying on the steps, wearing that jacket there. The thing's brain is so fried from riding the meths train all night, he's bladdy forgotten he's carrying stolen goods." Truter slapped the fender in delight. "So now my colleague must book him in for interrogation. I swear it's eyes the size of paper plates, and snot and trane as the vuil thing tells my colleague about coming face-to-face with a dead white man in a caravan." Truter gave the fender another appreciative slap. "Mense, this is why I love my career."

"What a story," said Meissner, in nervous admiration. "Where's he now?"

"Who?"

"The criminal."

"Ag, probly feeling all sorry for himself in a gutter somewhere. You chuck these things in the back of the van, leave them to cook in the sun, rock and roll them on a 4x4 road, and you think that will help them see right from wrong? Forget it! The second you dump them out in the veld, they're back to their old nonsense." Truter switched back to serious mode. "If you gentlemen will excuse me, I need to call my superior to organise a search warrant."

"A search warrant? For what?"

Truter aimed a pork sausage at the blue gum trees. "For that." His tone was cold and official. He was no longer leaning casually against the van. "The suspect in the aforementioned case has confessed breaking into that caravan and stealing that jacket." Truter lowered his hand towards his hip. "The South African Police Services have reasonable causes to believe there's a dead white man inside that alleged caravan." He stared grimly at the day's dying embers, allowing the gravity of the situation to take slow effect. The couple skulking behind Meissner stood rooted to the ground, pale and sick with terror. Meissner himself was shaking his head from side to side, struggling to grasp the dangerous unfolding reality.

Without any pre-emptive warning, Truter's hand came down on the van's bonnet like a thunderclap from the heavens.

"Fok, is that funny or what! Just imagine, Meissner, a white man sitting on ice in these people's nice Jurgens caravan. Not even I've seen that in my twenty-eight years in the force." He thumped Meissner on the back, rattling his implants. Meissner chortled nervously, in the manner of someone giving a crotch-sniffing Rottweiler a pat on the head. "That is a fine joke. That is a very fine joke you make, Sergeant."

"And you know what's a bigger lag, Meissner?"

"Ja?"

"If these people now have the white man's head in the coolbox, and have fed the rest of him to your biliary-infested brak here!"

32

After a long day trawling Rustenburg's old age homes for funeral kickbacks, Pastor Gerald Phelps of the North West New Evangelical Reform Church unlocked his front door and stepped into the homely smell of Mr Min and Cobra Floor Wax. It felt good to be home.

"Beauty?" he called down the hallway. "Beauty!"

A stern word would be called for in the morning, because this wasn't the first time the woman had left early. He ran his finger along the ball-and-claw sideboard and held it to the light; a well-trained domestic was near impossible to find these days.

Pulling off his white collar, he headed straight for the lounge. He flipped through the pile of mail left on the table, among it his monthly Capitec statement; the usual bulk meat specials from the Checkers Hyperama in Brits;

an Agri Festival flyer; and his Beares and Telkom account.

A stiff drink was calling his name. He dug out the key from behind his video collection, unlocked the cabinet, and screwed open the box tap, filling his glass with a "subtle fusion of youngberry and Marmite". He lowered himself into the couch and sighed contentedly.

For a modest man of the cloth, Phelps had done rather well for himself. Complementing the new Nevada lounge suite was a new glass-top coffee table, a new Hisense 60-inch plasma television with surround-sound speakers, and a new DSTV Explora decoder.

"What the hell?"

Phelps leant in for a better view, for a moment thinking he was imagining it. He stood up and walked over to the patio door. What in God's name was Beauty thinking? He pulled the patio door shut and toggled the key. Unbelievable! Not only had the woman left the door open, she had somehow managed to smash the lock. His blood boiled. His blood pressure spiked. Abandoning his efforts, Phelps slam-locked the Trellidor shut and padded over to the Salton; he'd hardly eaten a thing all day and was ravenous. One thing he'd grant that woman – at least she knew how to cook. He peeled away the clingwrap and surveyed the steaming heap of grilled lamb chops, sweet potato with sugar and cinnamon, buttered carrots, and yellow rice swimming in Knorr.

With the lamb chops sucked clean and his third glass of

Drostdy Hof coursing through the veins, Gerald Phelps felt like a new man. Lowering the volume on Stephanie Powers, he settled deeper into the Nevada and turned his attention to his mail.

A hundred and fifty bucks for ten kilos' pork mince wasn't a bad deal; a trip to Brits might be called for. He tore open the Telkom account: three hundred and eighty-four rand and fifty-four cents. Higher than usual and cause for concern. Either Beauty was using the phone, or Telkom was ripping him off. Or both. He reached over for his glass; for some reason the wine now tasted more Marmite than youngberry. And for some reason he felt queasy.

Phelps had kept the Capitec statement for last. It never ceased to amaze him how small amounts added up over time. What with the New Horizons funeral commissions and his TFS life cover loyalty credits, he would be back on his feet in no time. Phelps burped. Then burped again. He set the bank statement aside and rubbed his chest. The queasiness had upgraded to acute heartburn; that's what came from drinking on an empty stomach. His plans for a quiet evening in were dissolving rapidly, and the mere thought of watching flesh on flesh on the new Plasma was nauseating. His stomach cramped and roiled. The heartburn was unbearable. Phelps climbed unsteadily to his feet. This was pain of an entirely new order, as an unseen force took a long dagger to his bowels, twisting and turning it this way, then that way. His chest was swimming in pool acid. He couldn't decide if he needed to vomit, drop a load, or carry out both simultaneously. He staggered across the carpet towards the bathroom.

Gripping the toilet bowl, Phelps implored whoever above might be listening for blessed relief. His pleas were promptly answered with a fresh assault of nausea and cramping, the likes of which he had never before experienced.

Choking on his vomit, Pastor Gerald Phelps of the North West New Evangelical Reform Church collapsed face first to the floor. Less than a minute later, he was gone.

33

Tarryn Aldridge applied the lipstick in thick confident strokes. The name had grabbed her from word go: Summer Rouge – For the Woman Who Dares to be Different. She pouted Sophia Loren-like into the mirror. It tied in brilliantly with her highlights. She looked over her shoulder to check nothing was sticking out. She'd seen it for herself at the Ocean Basket in Gold Reef City – this quite pretty-looking woman coming out the loo dragging a long sheet of toilet paper behind her. You didn't get more embarrassing than that.

Tarryn packed away her lipstick and mascara stick in their little case, grabbed a last look in the mirror, then set off across the restaurant to join Steve at their table.

"How's your steak, babes?"

"Not bad. Your ribs look good?"

"They are. Especially with the monkeygland sauce. But I just wish they would turn the lights down. It's like a mortuary in here."

"At least we found somewhere to eat."

"That's true."

"How about we order another wine each? It's only twenty rand a glass."

"We should have ordered a bottle, to celebrate and all."

"Why celebrate?"

"You know, Stevie. Coming up with a solution to the problem this morning? Not panicking in front of that psycho cop?"

"I didn't think of it like that … We better keep it down – the waitress is coming."

"You people enjoying your meal?"

"It's nice, thanks. Can we order another glass of your house wine?"

"Same as last time. White and a red?"

"Yes, please."

"You want a doggy bag for that, ma'am?"

"I'm still busy."

"Okay, but shout if you do. So, where you guys from?"

"Sasolburg. We were—"

"We're on our way to Kruger," intercepted Tarryn.

"Why you staying here then? I would be like, head straight for Kruger. Don't pass Begin, don't collect two hundred rand."

"We enjoy touring," intercepted Tarryn again. "We like experiencing different parts of the country and all that."

"This place is a dump. I can't wait to get out."

"Why don't you leave then?"

Bianca – according to the badge on her shirt – rubbed two fingers together. "Don't you worry, as soon as I have the bucks I'm out of here big time."

"Aren't you married?" asked Tarryn.

Bianca held up her hand. "Do you see a ring? No ways, my boyfriend and me aren't into the whole society commitment marriage thing. I don't even know where he's at this very minute."

"What you mean?"

"Like, I mean he's gone AWOL. Disappeared without saying a word. I'm going to kill him when he gets back, because he mustn't think he can just come and go as he pleases ... Sorry, here I'm sharing my personal sob story. A white and a red coming up."

Tarryn waited until Bianca was back behind the bar. "Don't even go there, Steve."

"But you must be thinking what I'm thinking?"

"What, that it's one and the same?"

"It's possible, don't you think?"

"Anything's possible. There's also something called coincidence. People come and go all the time. And that's called life. Maybe you've heard of it? Shit, just when we were starting to relax." Tarryn tore at a rib.

"Sorry, but after that close shave with the policeman

this afternoon … Okay, maybe I'm just being paranoid."

Tarryn dipped her fingers into the water bowl and flicked them at her husband. "At least you're man enough to admit it."

"Hey, you do that again and I'll have no choice but to chuck you in the pool at Satara."

"I dare you. In fact, I can't wait."

Aldridge took a sip of wine. "You want to hear my idea, T?"

"Not another one. Okay, go ahead, tell me."

"I reckon one day we should sell the house and go live in the bush."

"And do what?"

"Manage a lodge or something. I could study game ranging through Unisa and take the tourists on guided drives and walks. And you could cook for them. You always said you wanted to own a restaurant."

"Sounds great, babes. You and your grand dreams – it's cute."

"If you don't have dreams, what do you have?"

"Maybe I'm not so keen on giving up our comforts and living in the jungle."

"It's not the jungle; it's—"

"You know what I mean. Anyway, how would we pay off the bond?"

"Like I said, we sell the house."

"Oh, ja? Even you said the Prinsloos struggled for months to sell their place before they went to New

Zealand."

"Australia."

"Same diffs."

"We would wait until the market improves and then sell. Seriously, I can see you running a restaurant or tea garden in the bush—"

"Talking about restaurants, what are we going to do about that potjie competition tomorrow? The guy was so pushy about us going. I can't stand him."

"I don't know if we have a choice, now that we're stuck here for another day. It might take our mind off things for a few hours, don't you think?"

"Maybe it will. Maybe it won't."

"I'm just trying to be positive."

"I know."

"And it's better than sitting around all day, worrying non-stop."

"S'pose so. But I'm not so sure I want to hang out with all these weird people." Tarryn took a sip. "This wine's going straight to my head. Not that I'm complaining; it's a nice feeling. Anyway, your choice."

"Could also be the wine, but I'm actually getting into the idea. You know, playing the locals at their own game, and all. You haven't forgotten the braai party we did for your thirtieth? How we cleaned up?"

"I forgot about that! I even won that bottle of JC Le Roux for the best marinade."

"Exactly. You and me were a hot team – Mr and Mrs

Braai Master. No reason we can't do it again. Come on, T, with your potjie sauce and my braai skills, we could do some serious damage." Aldridge took a large gulp of red. "Imagine ending on a high note like that?"

Tarryn stared dreamily out the window. At the empty parking lot. At the orange EXAS GRILL sign flickering above. "I hear what you're saying, babes. It would be amazing. We'll be like this Bonnie and Clyde couple riding off into the sunset. I so clean forgot about my thirtieth, but you're right, we can do this thing." Her eyes had glazed over.

"What you thinking now?"

"Nothing."

"Oh yes, you are … I know when you're scheming."

"I'm not scheming. I'm just thinking …" Tarryn held up her glass. "To us, Stevie. And to showing these people what we're made of."

34

Tertius Smit was in the mood for something romantic – a little sad maybe, but not too sad. He turned to his partner, who was relaxing in his father's old reading chair.

"How about Richard Clayderman? No? Okay, let me check now." He chose another album from the shelf under the television and held it up for her to see. "I bet you'll like

Kenny Rogers. He's from America, just like you."

Tertius removed the record from the sleeve and wiped it with the blue velvet cloth. He brushed the cloth against his cheek – it took him back to his childhood, to those afternoons with his mom on the couch, listening to her music while a Transvaal storm hammered down outside the window.

He lowered the needle. The sitting room crackled with static.

"May I have this dance, Savanna?" asked Tertius respectfully. He took the faintly surprised look on her face for a "Yes". He lifted her up from the chair and pulled her close to him. He felt the tension flow from his body. He buried his face in her sparkling fresh hair. It was so pure he could drink it.

Tertius and Savanna swayed gently to the music, lost in the loamy gravel of Kenny's voice.

Side Two had ended. The evening had flown by, but Tertius felt more awake, more alive than he'd felt in a long time. If it wasn't a week day, he would stay up the whole night, watch the sun rise over the—

Tearing himself from Savanna's peachy skin, he lowered her gently onto the couch, walked over to the record player, and lifted the needle.

"What you say we go for a drive to the end of the farm and watch the moon come over the koppie? You wanna do it, Sav?" He was getting into the American accent thing.

She naturally thought it a brilliant idea, because according to the label on the box, SAVANNA IS A FOXIE GIRL WHOSE ALWAYS UP TO TRYING NEW THINGS!! "Okay, that's fantastico. You wait here while I go get the bakkie keys."

A groom carrying his bride over the threshold, Tertius carried Savanna across the backyard to his Isuzu. She was so amazingly light – much lighter (and shorter, for that matter) than he had expected from the Miss America picture on the website. She was also so feminine. Not like the women at his church.

It was a beautiful evening, the air warm and still, the cicadas already out in force. He leant across and buckled her seat belt; accidents didn't only happen on tar roads.

Tertius reversed out the gate and dipped the headlights as they passed the granny flat of his tenants Gary Johnson and Bianca – he could never remember her surname, even though they had been living there now for more than three months. The bedroom light was on, the curtain half-open. Just past the cottage he cut a right onto a jeep track and entered the kloof. Tertius glanced across at Savanna; she was staring straight ahead with those wide blue eyes of hers, obviously enjoying the night tour of his farm. He was also enjoying himself – life was so much better when you had someone to share it with. He switched over to diff lock.

"Better hold on, Sav, this last part is a little bit bumpy." The Isuzu rumbled and lurched and worked its way

165

slowly up the koppie. According to his research on the subject, women were attracted to confident men who were in control. Tertius felt confident and in control. They crested the top of the koppie; an open patch of grassy ground appeared in the headlights. He switched off the engine and the lights, unbuckled Savanna, and pulled her over to him on the bench seat.

"That's what I call perfect timing," he whispered, pointing to the sliver of yellow crescent cutting the dark horizon. "I bet you've never seen one of these before? Watch, watch! Here she comes …" The couple gazed in silent awe as the full moon climbed the night sky and washed the maize fields below in silver. "Isn't that the most beautiful thing you've ever seen? My dad brought us here every time there was a full moon. As long as I live, I'll never stop appreciating it."

Stifling a yawn, he squeezed his California Babe closer to him and kissed her lightly on the cheek. Stroking her long blonde hair, he couldn't get over how lovely, silky, and soft it was. She was everything the website had promised. Everything and more.

He imagined Savanna stir sleepily against him. She wasn't one of those complainer types, but he could tell she was exhausted. Which was understandable, because she'd had a hell of a long journey. What with all the stress and worry collecting her from the post office that morning, he also now felt exhausted.

"Shall we go back?"

As Tertius turned the ignition, he realised there was no going back: he was fast falling for Savanna.

35

"Who the hell's that now?"

There was one thing Otto Meissner hated more than early arrivals – late arrivals. He flopped over on to his side and peered at the Hisense. "What psycho arrives at this crazy hour?"

"I'll go," said Susan Meissner, placing the DH Lawrence on the side table separating the beds, and wrapping her shawl around her.

Meissner pulled his blanket higher. "You sure?"

"Yes, Otto, I'm sure." She dug her Japanesey numbers from under the bed and padded out the room.

"And tell them we're not a bus station!" muttered Meissner behind her, before shovelling his bulk deep into the covers.

Susan walked down the passage, praying the knocking hadn't woken the stressed-out couple from Sasolburg. Ahead, a tall silhouette loomed large through the brown stippled glass. She unlocked the Trelli Slamlock, pulled the top and bottom latches and unlocked the front door. A tanned specimen with chiselled jaw and a sheen of thick black hair combed back towered above her. He was dressed in a denim jacket, black T-shirt, and jeans tucked into leather boots. The smile was sheepish, lopsided and punctuated by an Arnold Schwarzenegger gap between white teeth. A duffel bag hung over his left shoulder. For some strange reason, Susan Meissner couldn't help but note these myriad details.

"Flip, I'm sorry for arriving in the middle of the night like this. I tried to phone on the road, but by the time I got reception I was already here."

Susan Meissner pulled the shawl tighter to her body. "Really, it's not a problem. I'm glad you've arrived safe."

"Me too. It's good to be here at last." He extended a hand. A strong tanned hand. "Sorry, I'm forgetting my manners. The name's Angel. Johnny Angel. I think it must have been your manager I booked with this morning."

"My husband. Is that all your luggage?"

"Yip. Travelling light."

"We have you booked in our garden cottage, if that's okay?"

"At this stage of the night, a bus shelter would be okay." He laughed. A deep manly laugh. He reached into his jacket pocket. "You want me to pay you now?"

"No, really, you can pay when you check out. Let's go through the house; it's quicker."

Susan Meissner led the way through the lounge and into the kitchen, out the back sliding doors, down the side alley of the house, past the fibreglass plunge pool and washing line, and across Otto's pride and joy patch of lawn, to

Buffalo Suite – in reality less his advertised Luxurious Singles Apartment than reincarnated Verwoerd-era domestic worker's room attached to the back of the garage.

"Sorry it's so dark. There's a step coming up."

"No worries, I've got cat eyes."

Susan Meissner could well believe it – there was something distinctly lion about him." Which explained, or didn't explain the raised hairs on her neck.

"Let me help you there, ma'am."

"Susan. Thank you. My husband hasn't yet got around to fixing the lock. Are you here on business?"

"Yep. Industrial cleaning chemicals is my game. Voila! Open Sesame."

Susan brushed past Johnny Angel and switched on the light. "It's nothing fancy, but hopefully you'll be comfortable—"

"Hey, no need to apologise all the time. It's perfect. So many nice little touches. Even fresh flowers, nogal."

Susan Meissner felt her face warm. She tucked a wayward lock of hair behind her ear and turned to leave.

"Well, I hope you have a good night. And … maybe we'll see you for breakfast in the morning."

"Don't you worry, I'm gonna crash like a HiAce on the N1. You've been very kind, Susan."

"Only a pleasure, Mr Angel."

"Johnny."

"Sorry, Johnny."

Johan Engelbrecht latched the door and surveyed the lie of the land. Three-quarter bed with duvet and single pillow in the centre of the room. Toilet and shower through curtain on the right. Four times glass containers marked Tea, Coffee, Sugar, Cremora. Two mugs – one of them chipped – and a stainless-steel milk jug on a tray. A thirty-two-inch TV suspended on a bracket in the corner. Buffalo Suite? It would do for a night or two. Three max. He walked over to the kitchenette counter and switched on the kettle.

Engelbrecht lifted his duffel bag onto the bed, unzipped it, and pulled out his briefcase. He flipped open the lid. The contents included an iPad, his Global Clean Flipfile, a ring-bound black notebook, and his 9mm revolver – so far it hadn't come to it, but one could never be sure what was waiting around the next corner. Engelbrecht powered up the iPad and opened his Excel spreadsheet. He checked his phone. No missed calls or SMS from Cynthia. The waiting around was sending his brain into overdrive.

He lay back on the bed, his head against the wall, stewing over the facts at hand. He had stumbled upon something earlier at that dodge New Horizons operation – his gut told him as much – but like a bar of Lifebuoy in the bath, he couldn't get a grip on it. It had been the same old story for weeks now – goose-chasing a trail that went from cold to lukewarm, then back to cold. He had already forgotten how long he'd been chasing the tail of this thing; it was one fat blur with nothing solid to show except a pile of stats and correlations that pointed to a shit stink of note. But no smoking gun or body in the gutter. He scrolled down the spreadsheet; it wasn't telling him anything new. Little wonder that BEE prick Duminy was getting all heavy with him, threatening to pull the case. The guy was nothing but a messenger boy for the SAPS fat cats sitting in their aircon offices, with their Virgin Active secretaries buzzing around them like flies on shit.

Engelbrecht got up and switched off the kettle. He was no longer lus for coffee. Especially crap instant with Cremora. He turned off the light and stretched out on the bed, breathing deeply, trying to relax. Deep down, lurking somewhere between conscious and subconscious, something was telling him *something*. His legs twitched restlessly under him. This time it was different. The loose and broken bits — they were starting to form a pattern. He couldn't yet see it, but he could *feel* it.

Day 3

36

Truter approached the Brits Municipality building from the west, from the Checkers Hyperama side. A square grey block running seven storeys high, it reminded him of his old hunting grounds at John Vorster Square – cock on block, it was one and the same builder who had squirrelled up the arses of Magnus and PW. Truter spat onto the pavement, expunging the bitter aftertaste that came with memory. The day was fast coming when he would resign from the force and start his own private security business and do things his way. The right way.

He had planned the op well. Like any muni on an early Saturday morning, the place was near deserted. A grizzled Fidelity security guard dozed in the sun on a plastic garden chair near the front entrance. Truter stepped past him and trundled up the stairs to the revolving door, pausing to admire the fine figure reflecting back at him – in its blue church suit and size-fourteen brown Hush Puppies.

Stepping into the foyer, Truter breathed in the combo of Cobra wax, Jeyes fluid, and old sweat – government places all smelled the same. He scanned the board above the abandoned reception desk, mouthing the names as he worked his way down. Midway through the second column, he found what he was looking for: Suite B4. Since when was a normal office no longer good enough for a mayor?

He was taking a fat chance, but it was now or never. For the past twenty-four hours he had been pulled along by a giant invisible magnet, and there was no stopping it now. The Whys and Whats and the connections between recent events were still little more than loose thoughts banging around his head like heavy items in a washing machine. Freddie and Dippies pitching up together at Texas Grill after twenty-five years? Bang! Freddie's and Jakkals's and Connie Botes's name on that insurance form of Ferdie Meyer? Bang! That OPENING SPEECH BY BRITS MAYOR, JAKKALS D VENTER Prestik'd to the window at the Check-In when he went to buy his mom's groceries? Bang! Although lacking coherent shape or form or causal relation, something deep and primal within Truter had sniffed a rat. And when Clinton Truter sniffed a rat, not even a hosepipe up the backside would get him to let go.

Gripping the official folder he had borrowed from Delport's desk, he strolled casually down the corridor –

like any other upstanding member of the community on official duty – and studied the floor. It was the usual grey linoleum, but not the high gloss like in the old days; this one was lifting at the corners and gatvol. He passed an open office door; a bored face stared back at him from behind its desk. He had reached the end of the corridor. So far, so good. The stairs were to the right.

Arriving at the second floor, he stopped at the window to regroup and catch his breath. His heart was now pumping, his hands cold and clammy. He took in the view over Brits – brown, moth-eaten veld and depressing buildings slowly disappearing back into the earth. Ashes to ashes. Dust to dust. It was the law of the universe according to Ross the Toss, his ex-brother-in-law. Entropy, or something hyperluted like that, was what he called it. That's what happened when you cut Three Ships with rotgut – you fried your brain.

B1 came up first. Then B2. B4 beckoned ahead. But now a serious problem was heading his way: a dressed-for-a-wedding secretary-looking woman in high heels carrying a pile of papers. Truter retreated back to the window and studied Delport's folder. Glancing sideways, he sized up the quarry – one of those New South Africa women he'd seen in Joburg, with their fancy cellphones and wallets stuffed with Edgars and Jet Store cards. A white chick would never go to the same trouble to look that good, unless it was her own wedding she was going to – Sharon a case in point.

Truter's heart pounded as the woman pulled up in front of B4 and started rattling through a bunch of keys. She turned and smiled at him. A lone old lion roaming the drought-ridden plains of Africa, Truter made his move.

"Mevrou, let me help you there!" he said, shimmying across the linoleum and plucking the bunch from her hand, and taking note of the wedding ring and stone the size of a rock.

"Wow, thanks so much."

"No problemo. You must be the only one here working on a Saturday. You work for the mayor?"

"Just helping out until Mr Venter's assistant gets back from sick leave." She spoke like those hot chicks on *Days of Our Lives*.

"And Mr Venter? Is he not coming in today?"

"As far as I know, he's attending an official event."

"Got you." Truter had manoeuvred himself into position: back to the woman, front facing Venter's door and the gold plaque square-on. "Okie dokes, let's see what's going on here." Keeping the conversation ticking over like a diesel bakkie on a winter's morning, he sorted through the bunch, "Let us try M30. Nope! Maybe it's this one, H18. Nope! Not H18 either." He inserted M2B. "Voilas!" He unlocked the door and stepped aside. "All yours, madam. Take your time, while I sort out this key mess for you."

"Are you sure? It's so kind of you."

"If we can't help each other in this country, who can we

help then?"

"Well, in that case, thanks. But I won't be a sec."

Truter moved back into the passage, flicking through the bunch. There was only one M2B. Which left him with only one option.

"Looks like I'm all done," the Days of Our Lives said from behind him. "Thank you again for being so helpful."

"No worries. I'll lock up for you, because I bet you want to get home and enjoy the weekend with your family?" She had nice eyes. And perfect white teeth. And Cadbury's milk chocolate skin.

"I am actually looking forward to knocking off."

"Exactly." Replanting himself back in front of the door, Truter turned the key to the right, then back to the left, while simultaneously clearing his throat of phlegm. He turned and handed the bunch of keys to the Days of Our Lives. "After you, mevrou." Like the true gentleman he was, he insisted she walk ahead of him.

37

Otto Meissner sat at his desk. Gloating. Stroking his paunch. Savouring the warm fuzzy feeling of success. Luck hadn't got him to this point. A rare combination of talent, skill, and vision had. The vision to spot and seize an opportunity by the jugular when it came his way. In fact, he had just recently come to realise he shared a lot in common with that other business visionary and great human being: Donald J Trump.

A swarm of ideas had been following in the wake of his breakfast chat with the Galactic Tours chappie. He could just see it – American tourists arriving in their droves in Kombi buses. Why he hadn't seen it before, the North West's massive potential, was a little beyond him. But now that Abrahams had pointed it out, it was so obvious – the province was about to explode. And the thing Abrahams said about the government having to build more airports to handle the extra load? That was proof in the pudding.

A lizard-like tongue darted across Meissner's Highveld-parched lips. He already had his strategy worked out: he would play it nice and slow with the Galactic rep, soften him up, keep up the wining and dining and charming the pants off him. Then, when he was least expecting it, he would strike like a cobra!

Fifteen years in the B&B game had taught Meissner a thing or two about human nature. He could tell a mile away that Abrahams was a big shot at Galactic; a director at the very least. The story about the helicopter rescue in the Alps was a dead giveaway, because there was no ways in hell HQ would send a heli to rescue a lowly sales rep – even if an avalanche was about to flatten the resort. This was all the more reason why he had to play it nice and slow with the guy. By the time his replacement Avis car pulled up the driveway, Abrahams would be begging one Otto

Horst Meissner to sign on the dotted line. It would be like that *Reader's Digest* story, about the plumber in America who saved a millionaire's daughter from drowning, and ended up inheriting the millionaire's fortune after he died in a car crash three months later.

Meissner reached across the desk for his calculator. Three Ships x three triples: R150. Side bowl of peanuts and a biltong stick: R45. Rhino Room x one night: R650. Full Eden buffet breakfast x 1: R75. A few brandy-and-Cokes and a toasted chicken mayo later at the plunge pool, the meter would be hitting a thousand rands before lunch – excluding mini-bar. Like he'd read in *Art of the Deal*, and like he'd told his wife, you had to spend money to make money. She would be thanking him big time when the bucks started rolling in from Galactic Tours (Pty) Ltd and its associate companies: White Lion Breeding Farms (Pty) Ltd and White Lion Hunting Safaris (Pty) Ltd.

Meissner leant back in the chair and gloated some more. Stroked his paunch some more, enjoying the cotton rubby feeling. His ISM with Abrahams – Investment Strategy Meet – had gone well. Fantastically well. He had kept his cards close to his chest, played hardball when he had to, pretended not to be interested when he had to, acted like it was just casual chit-chat when he had to. Meanwhile, back at the ranch, he was strategising big time, running circles around Abrahams, prepping him for the kill. Meissner chuckled at the fresh memory; by the time they'd agreed on his first ten thousand cash instalment to White Lion

Breeding Farms, the man was tripping all over himself to tie up the deal.

Pulling open the desk drawer, he scratched around for his bunch of master keys. He had already decided he would start small, with no more than four, maybe five Eden Palms in the North West – all of them near the lion-breeding operations – before rolling out his franchise to the rest of the country. Controlling his excitement with a long deep breath, he checked his watch – by now Abrahams would have cashed his cheque and made the deposit into the investment consortium's account. But like he had told him straight, it was his way or the highway: the consortium would get the other twenty thousand when his overdraft was approved. Because nobody, but nobody, told Otto Meissner what to do.

38

With a view over the Hyperama and a gold coat of arms dead centre in a red wall-to-wall carpet, he had to hand it to the old fox: Jakkals had outdone himself getting into the hen house.

Truter stood at the door, admiring the plush trappings that came with the title of Brits mayor. The office was something out of *Dallas*, with a dark wood desk the size of a minibus taxi parked in front of the window, and a black-

and-chrome leather chair pulled up behind it. A wall of (empty) book shelves with fancy glass doors filled the one wall. Built into the bookshelf was a drinks cabinet with an automatic pouring thingie and posh glasses arranged on a silver tray – exactly like JR's office.

A ratel drawn to a bee hive, Truter headed straight for the drinks cabinet. He pulled the stopper from the empty decanter and took a sniff. Martell VOC? Or even something grander.

He moved around Venter's desk and rolled out the chair. He could tell Jakkals had a squad of secretaries doing his work, because there was hardly anything on the desk. He lifted a framed photo and studied it – a young-looking Jakkals and his wife and their two kids on a speedboat smiled grimly back at him. Behind them the water was white with chop. Looking past the droopy tits in the bikini top, she was okay in the looks department – he wouldn't say no if it came to it. He set the photo down and inspected the other items on the desk. An In/Out tray with some papers; a TFS calendar; a black glass ashtray filled with crushed stompies; a mini clock; a Perspex box filled with pens and pencils and a carved ivory letter opener.

Truter manoeuvred himself into the chair and got comfy. He pushed back on it, swivelled to the left, swivelled to the right. It was like driving a Rolls Royce. He pulled open the top drawer. The usual man-drawer: loose paper clips; an old Autobank card; a BIC lighter; a half-eaten Tex Bar; a tube of Mycota squeezed dry; leaking

AAA batteries and loose keys; a wad of business cards held together with elastic bands; a pack of open Carlton men's tissues; a cellphone charger; a tube of Vicks lip ice.

He leaned down and slid open the second drawer. It was even less interesting. Nothing but coloured folders marked Brits Municipality this and that. All of them admin. Truter flipped through the contents, clueless what he was looking at – he should have brought Delport. Then again, maybe not.

Same again with the last drawer. Nothing but bladdy admin. He shoved it back in and sat back, drumming his fingers on the black leather armrests. He hadn't woken at sparrow's fart and driven two hours for nothing. There had to be something more. Anything.

A nauseous pit with no name had now taken up residence in Truter's gut. It was like Jakkals was in the room with him. *In* the collapsed leather of the chair. In the *smell* coming off the Chesterfield stompies and stale carpet. He could see him standing at the drinks cabinet, his staunch legs wide apart, pouring his rum and Coke. Truter reached across the desk for the photo. Except for the extra weight, Jakkals hadn't changed much. Always that same sideways look with the jaw pushed out, and the ice-blue eyes that cut through you like a blade. Truter pushed the photo away, as if it had come suddenly to writhing life in his hands. He shut his eyes, trying to remember, at the same time trying to forget that night at The Farm. Trying to remember exactly what went down. Trying *not* to remember the smell of rubber and burning flesh and the manic laughing mixed in with the moaning coming from inside the workshop. Trying *not* to remember Jakkals's calm voice in his ear, telling him it was going to be okay, as long as he kept his mouth shut—

Truter's phone was vibrating in his pocket. Delport! The moegoe really knew how to choose his moment. Bugger him! The mission was going nowhere fast. According to the desk clock, he'd been staring out like a zombie for the past ten minutes. Any moment Days of Our Lives was going to bang down the door. PING! What now? He pulled the Nokia from his pocket and scrolled through Delport's SMS.

RE. MISSING PERSON, SIR. ANONYMOUS PHONE CALL RECEIVED. WITNESS SAW MAN CARRYING BODY. LOCATION: FARM NOOIT VERDRIET. WITNESS HAS IDENTIFIED SUSPECT.

Truter smiled grimly. Nice one, Delport. This was the breakthrough he'd been waiting for. He typed back:

aM on mY way. We HAV Our man!!!!

A pit bull locked onto the throat of a Maltese, Truter wasn't quite ready to let go. At the very least he deserved a souvenir to take home from his undercover mission. He eyed the empty bookcase and drinks cabinet across the room. The decanter would look good in his flat, but too risky. Pulling out the top drawer, he again rummaged through the contents, sifting through the keys and business cards and paper clips and sweet wrappers and pocket calculator and Mycota tube and pack of postage stamps and mini Lunch Bar and … a Transcend computer stick hiding right at the back, which he hadn't noticed before. Truter knew it was a computer stick because Delport had one just like it to back up the office computer files – or something to that effect. The polyester of Truter's trousers stiffened as a thought floated into view – the stick might be filled with porno. He wouldn't put it past Jakkals. And it wouldn't be the usual tame stuff. It would be hard core as all hell.

Giving the subject no further thought, Truter dropped the computer stick and the Lunch Bar into his jacket pocket, then as an afterthought added the ivory letter opener. He closed the drawer and angled the photo to face forwards. He stood up and rolled the chair back into its position. Satisfied, he walked over to the door and pressed his ear against the mahogany veneer. Slowly opening the door, he peered up and down the corridor. All clear. He turned, gave the royal den a final look-over, then stepped into the passage, pulling the door behind him. Home and a missing person's interrogation were calling his name.

39

Sucking hard on the Camel Plain, Johan Engelbrecht contemplated the dust bowl below – South African platteland at its ugly best. It was places like this, not the cities, where Africa's soul throbbed hardest under its thin skin of respectability. This was where Engelbrecht felt most alive, where his skin tingled at the possibilities. It was Bloedrivier in the making all over again – jumpy whites surrounded by encroaching squatter sprawl. All it needed was a match.

Engelbrecht flipped open his cellphone and hit speed dial. He leant back against the black Subaru. "Take It Easy" floated out the open window.

"Well, I'm running down the road trying to loosen my load, I've got a world of trouble on my mind … Sorry, howzit, Cynth! How things going up there? … Ja, same old, just another day in paradise … Listen, sweetie pie, I don't want to hak, but did you manage to pull anything for me yet?" Engelbrecht flicked the Camel to the ground and crushed it under his boot. The ex was right; smoking was a filthy habit. "Sorry, can you speak a bit louder, this line's seriously kak … Okay, that's better. Let's start with this Mitchell boytjie … You did? Go girl! … Ja, it has to be him. I mean, how many other Glen Mitchells can there be in the province? And can you see on the system when he signed up?" Engelbrecht released a long slow

whistle. "Jesus, that's not even six months. Just a sec …"
He waited for the abattoir truck at the bottom of the hill
to pass. He could see straight into it – a shaggy carpet
of sheep on a one-way picnic outing. "You've seriously
made my day, Cynth. Okay, I'm pushing it here, but did
you manage to find anything on whatshisname … Roger
Henley? Tell me I'm wrong but I reckon there's something
not kosher with that asthma story …. Are you serious?
Shit, now you've made my flipping month."

One connection he would have been satisfied with, but
hitting the Lotto twice on the same day, it was more than
Engelbrecht had dared to hope for. He reached into the
car. "I better write this down … Go for it – 13 March.
What year? … Unfokkenbelievable." He scribbled some
more. "I have to double-check on my computer but looks
like the turnaround time is getting shorter." Below the
koppie and the MTN tower, the dust bowl was stirring
into life. Humans coming out their houses. Cars starting
to move. An angle grinder starting up in the far distance.
He checked the time. "Listen, sweetie pie, I have to hit the
road, but I'll give you a buzz later. And you'll let me know
if anything comes in from West Rand side? … Perfecto.
One more thing, tell that slacker husband of yours I'm
inviting you guys and Tony and them for a skilpad braai
when I get back … AKA min vleis, baie dop. All right,
Cynth, we'll talk later. Ciao!"

Engelbrecht snapped his phone shut. He wasn't going
to jump the gun – not like the last goose chase after that

Pinnacle Insurance operation. But now suddenly all the signs were pointing in the same direction – to a hornet's nest of note. And this time he wasn't imagining it.

His hand started heading towards his pocket – the moment called for a celebratory Camel – then thought better of it. Like the ex said at every opportunity, there was nothing more disgusting than the smell of stale ash in a car, his or anybody else's. A Nicorette would have to do instead.

Engelbrecht started up the Subaru, gunned the engine, cranked up the volume on "Hotel California", and slammed the gear into reverse. It was time to bring the local boys in blue in on the game.

40

Parked deep under the blue gum trees, the yellow Hummer's mags shimmered in the morning sun. Behind the tinted windows, the four occupants stared out grimly at the human trickle meandering towards the entrance of the Agricultural Showgrounds. The atmosphere in the cabin was heating up; Jakkals Venter was in a tetchy mood.

"All right, one of you explain to me this David Copperfield magic trick, because I don't get it. How does someone sommer vanish into thin air? Dippies?"

Juan Dippenaar gazed sullenly through the backseat

window, tracking his wife and the kids. "I don't know, sir."

"You hear that, manne? 'I don't know, sir.' Not what I want to hear! Freddie, you say you double-checked the body shops and hospitals. What about the provincial in Brits?"

"Yebo. Everything inside a hundred and fifty-kay radius. Not once, but twice, Jakkie."

"Including the AVBOBs and all the other private morgues?"

"Including the AVBOBS and all the private morgues, Jakkie."

"Okay, okay, just making sure." Jakkals tugged at his ear. He drummed on his fur-clad steering wheel. He was thinking hard.

"What if someone's on to us?"

Freddie Ferreira rolled his eyes. "Ag, kom nou, Dippenaar. Where do you come with stront like that?"

"Maybe he has a point?"

"Like how, Jakkie? If someone was onto us, I promise you, we'd know all about it."

Dippenaar continued to look out the window; some overweight woman and her langderm husband had now ambushed Renate. "How would we know about it?"

"Hey, look a man in the eye when you have something to say."

Dippenaar turned back from the window. "Sorry, Jakkals."

"And don't keep fokken apologising. I swear, I'm up to

here with you lot."

"For ages now, Jakkals, I've been telling Freddie and the others we've been getting too windgat with this thing. Especially Freddie. Half the time he acts like it's a big joke."

Ferreira stared up at the flashing LED lights running the perimeter of the Hummer's ceiling. "Is that now right? Classic Dippies or what, Jakkie? From day dot, always looking for someone or *something* to blame. Remember that time we flipped the boat on the Cunene?"

Conrad Botes sniggered alongside. "I'll never forget that."

"Well?"

"Well, what, Freddie?"

"You remember whose fault it was, according to Mr Paranoid here?"

"Yours, Freddie."

"Exactly, Connie. And, Jakkals, you remember that saga about the Muslim conspiracy to take our farms for their Al Qaeda training camps? And now, out the blue someone's on to us – plus, I'm the cause of this oke disappearing."

"Easy, Freddie," cautioned Jakkals.

Ferreira tapped on the tinted window. "By the way, Dippies, nice new double cab you have standing there. May I ask where you got the cash from? Wesbank? I don't think so."

"That's telling him," wheezed Conrad Botes. He poked Dippenaar in the ribs. "Come on, boet, you must lighten up. Freddie, move up a bit your side; I can hardly breathe."

"Okay, manne, let's all calm down and sniff the coffee," said Jakkals. "Who's ready for a refill?" He shifted his bulk to the left and peered into the mini-bar fridge. "This ice-maker's a piece of kak; the stuff's still mushy. Pass me your cups."

Ferreira handed the paper cups to the front. "I am calm, Jakkie, but when certain no-names-mentioned individuals question the quality of my work, that's when I get pissed off big time. How many policies have I sold over the past month? Ten? Twenty? Lemme tell you. Thirty-six and counting! Here I'm working my arse off—"

Jakkals handed Ferreira and Botes their Martell. "I know that, Freddie, and I appreciate what you're doing. And the guys and their families appreciate it. Not so, manne? Good. So we all agree we're a bit jumpy, because of this latest event. But I stem saam with Freddie. If you're gonna grab at conclusions, Dippies, you better back it up with facts, not rumours. You hear me?"

"I was just saying—"

"And, Conrad, you can chuck that grin of yours out the window. We're all in this together. One for all, and all for one." Jakkals swallowed hard. Grimaced. "But Dippies is right about one thing: we're racing ahead of ourselves." He raised a finger, bringing Ferreira's objection to a skidding halt. "I'm not saying we're reckless or windgat. I'm saying we're moving too fast. It's become too easy. And when things become too easy, you have to be double alert to

danger, otherwise you're gonna land yourself in the kak."
Venter stared pensively into the empty cup. "Don't forget
where we've come from, manne. Don't forget those times
when things turned on their arse just like that." He clicked
his fingers.

"Like Operation Hyena, Jakkie?"

Jakkals winced, as if he needed the reminder. "Exactly,
Conrad. Perfect example. You onthou how for three
days straight we had the enemy on the run, like it was
open hunting season. Track. Contact. Track. Contact.
Every few hours, bam-bam! Bam-bam-bam, thank you,
ma'am," staccato'd Jakkals, picking off a group of blue-
overall labourers struggling under the weight of a chest
freezer. His voice dropped to a whisper. "And then what
happened? Fok, I still get the night sweats over it."

"Things went south, Jakkie."

"That's correct, Juan. Things went south. Out of the
sky, the situation switches one-eighty degrees and we're
running for our lives, seeing our arses big time." Jakkals
sighed heavily. "Six good men. Gone. Forever ... Anyways,
who needs another dop?"

"I won't say no, Jakkals."

"Me two."

"Me three."

The mood in the Hummer had turned solemn. Jakkals
lifted his cup. "To fallen comrades."

Ferreira, Botes, and Dippenaar lifted their paper cups.
"To fallen comrades."

41

Tertius Smit was facing a serious dilemma: confess to a crime he didn't commit or own up to the truth and face even worse consequences. Inferring from the blue riot boot pressing down on his cheek, of one thing he was certain: he was dead on either charge. One: The boot's owner would not take lightly to a confession of sexual depravity with a blow-up doll. Two: Confessing to the alleged charge of murdering a diabetic jogger and burying the body on his farm was also out of the question.

Above him, the source of his pain shifted its weight. Flashes of white light strobed across Smit's brain, and his crumpled face contorted further into something closely resembling a Shar Pei.

The policeman's questioning had now entered its second hour, with no let-up in sight. For the past sixty minutes, Smit had not only bounced off the walls, and rolled and scrambled across the floor, but twice he had been trapped in the scrum without oxygen, and then punted over the pale. The man was now preparing to ruck him from yet another loose maul.

"Come now, Smittie, you must also do your bit for the team," wheezed his interrogator, applying further pressure to the neck. A bubble of snot appeared at Smit's left nostril, inflated, then popped like a balloon at a kid's party.

His eyes bulged. "You ready for some more, because this is just the curtain raiser, my friend." With a feeble flap of his left arm – one of few limbs still capable of movement – Smit indicated in the negative. Again, his tormentor shifted position, bringing Smit nose-to-wiry-mass-of-black-hair sprouting from an inner thigh. A heady cocktail of overripe Camembert and stale urine descended from above.

Heaving like a bull, the policeman rolled off Smit.

Tertius Smit lay on his back, staring up at the water stain on the ceiling, unable to move, his body a broken sack of jelly, his bones crushed to powder. "Please, I'll tell you anything you want."

Sergeant Truter rubbed his aching knee. "I knew you would see the light, Smittie. You want to know why? Because you come from a good family. So … where's the body? You can tell—"

Constable Delport was standing at the door, looking a lighter shade of his usual pale, his face not quite comprehending, as if unable to place the sweat-soaked scene on the raw concrete floor in the New South Africa.

"What the hell is it, Delport? Can't you see I'm busy!"

"Sorry for interrupting, sir, but there's someone here to see you."

"So what! Tell them to fokken wait until I'm finished."

"I don't think they … he can wait. He says he's an agent from Special Crimes Unit in Pretoria."

It was Truter's turn to switch a shade of pale. "Special

Crimes Unit?" He attempted to stand up. "Help me, Delport; this bladdy knee of mine …" Pulling on Delport's arm for leverage, Truter staggered onto his feet and straightened up. He tucked in his shirt and wiped the sweat from his face. "How do I look?"

"Fine, sir, except for … around your mouth. I have a tissue if you want?"

Truter accepted Delport's tissue. "Is it all gone?"

"Yes, sir."

"Special Crimes Unit, you say?" Truter ran a hand through his hair. "This is all I need. Where's he now?"

"Waiting in your office. You want me to offer him a cup of coffee while you get ready?"

"Ja, whatever. Just … Just tell him I will be there in a few minutes. Tell him I'm busy on an important missing person's matter … Do we still have those Lemon Creams?"

"I think we do, sir."

"Feed him some of those to keep him occupied."

"Good idea."

Truter glared at his deputy. "So, what the hell you waiting for?"

"What about him?"

Truter had already forgotten about the interrogation. He turned to the murder suspect, who had in the interim crawled unnoticed into the far corner and was staring up at him like a traumatised nagapie. "I'll be dealing with you later, Smittie, but let me just say one thing. If your dad was still alive, he would very disappointed in you. Very disappointed." With a semblance of regained composure, Truter turned back to his deputy. "While you're at it, Delport, give Smit here a cup of tea. With extra sugar."

Truter's brain was now looping back and forth, firing off questions like random anti-aircraft into the night sky. What the hell was SCU doing in Edendal? Internal investigation! What else could it be? Why else would they send an agent all the way from Pretoria? He suddenly remembered the pages he'd ripped from his charge book. Fok! What if the guy demanded to check the station's records? How was he going to explain that one? These agents were a law unto themselves. They did as they pleased; they didn't need a search warrant ... His skin now turned cold. The hair on the back of his neck stood erect. It was the mountain of unsolved case files sitting on his filing cabinet – that's what SCU had come for! Destroying evidence was one thing, but failure to perform one's duty was a criminal offence. He let out a deep animal groan; the agent was digging in the files that very minute.

With no longer an inkling of doubt in Truter's mind that this was a sting operation, the sequence of events was clear as day. One. Special Crimes had been tipped off about the bribery-and-corruption and professional negligence going down at SAPS Edendal. Two. SCU were here to do a forensic audit of the station's finances, case files, and petty cash book. Three. His and Delport's arrest would follow immediately after.

Things were not looking good. Not good at all.

42

Back behind the Hummer's tinted windows, Jakkals Venter was now on a roll.

"Don't get me wrong, manne, this op is a wet dream come true. We're all making more bucks than we know what to do with. We're driving new cars. We're giving the wives overseas trips and fancy jewellery. We have holiday houses all over the country – Marloth Park, Stilbaai, Hartbeespoort, you name it. But we *have* to be careful. Ons moet paraat bly. Ons moet die disiplin hou. And … and we must learn our lesson from this Johnson boytjie. You all agree?" Ferreira, Dippenaar, and Botes nodded in unison from the back seat. "In ander woorde, we have to regroup and consolidate. Secondly, we must learn to put our feet up once in a while. The business isn't going to sommer evaporate if we take our foot off the pedal. We've been going at this thing hard for how long now? Freddie?"

"You mean from the first client?"

"Ja."

"Nearly ten years, Jakkie."

"You hear that? Nearly ten years. For ten years the business model has been rock solid. We have a moerse good team with a great skill set. Our costs are under control. The profit margin is sitting at where? Freddie?

"Sixty-five per cent."

"Sixty-five per cent! That's way higher than even my white lion operation. We're cruising, manne. So, please, I beg you, let's not mess up by being slapgat. You agree, Connie?"

"Ja, Jakkie."

"Hey, don't give me that *Ja, Jakkie, no, Jakkie, three bags full, Jakkie*. I want you to agree because you understand what I'm saying."

"I understand and I agree, but we also can't lie around at home twiddling our thumbs." Botes looked to Ferreira and Dippenaar for support. "We've all got bills to pay. You don't want to know what my new place on the Vaal is costing every month. I'll be sweating out my ring if the cash stops flowing."

"You're not listening, Conrad. Did I say the word *Stop*? Who heard me say *Stop*? See. Nobody. What I'm saying is we ease up and take hold of the situation." Venter crushed the paper cup in his fist and jammed it into the Hummer's mug holder. His jaw tightened. "Enough sweet talk. Let's get one thing straight here. Until you find this boytjie, dead or alive, I'm pulling all further ops. For fuck sakes, where's your pride! Lemme ask you something. Would you go hunting at Vaalwater, shoot a kudu, and then not track it? No, you wouldn't. If it took you all day and night you would track that bastard until you found it. You wouldn't just shrug your shoulders, reload, and take down another kudu. Am I right, or am I right?"

"You're right, Jakkals."

"No diffs then with this latest situation on our hands. We keep looking until we get to the bottom of it; I don't care how long it takes. Freddie, how much is the expected return on this one?"

"Five hundred and fifty grand, give or take a few for the next of kin. I must still work out the exact figures."

Venter pushed back into the leather bucket seat and stared through the windscreen at the crowds starting to move in. "I rest my case. Five hundred and fifty thousand bucks down the drain if we don't wrap it up." He shifted his gaze to the rear-view mirror. "Anything else on the agenda? Freddie?"

"All good my side."

"And you two? How did it go with client Henley and Mitchell?"

"Like a hot knife through margarine, Jakkals."

"That's more like it, Connie."

"Except ... a tiny thing with the predikant has come up."

Venter winced. He had never felt good about this one: religion and business weren't a good mix. "A tiny thing, what? You saying there's a problem?"

"No problem. It's just that they want to do a second autopsy."

"What are you telling me? And who's 'they'?"

"Don't worry, Jakkals, it's under control. It's just a formality. The family—"

"Fok, as if I don't have enough worries on my plate.

What you mean it's under control? It's only under control when he's under six feet of North West earth."

"Like I said, it's just a formality. Sometimes the family wants a second opinion. I've got my buddy at State Pathology doing the paperwork. He'll sort it out chop-chop and then we're good to go again."

"I told you we should have handled him the normal way," muttered Dippenaar into his Martell.

"Here we go again. Do you always have to be such be a dipshit? I said it's a bladdy formality. Even if they cut him open ten times, they wouldn't find a thing."

"Nice one, Con. Dippies the dipshit. That's funny, hey, Jakkals?"

"Ja, fokken hilarious. I'll take your word for it, Connie, but just make sure you sort it out pronto. Anyways, what's the time?"

"Almost twelve."

"Kak in a bucket! I have to work on my speech. We'll finish this conversation before I head back to Brits later. In the meantime, I want you boys to chill out, have a koeksuster, enjoy the potjie, spend quality time with your wife and kids. Act normal! You especially, Dippies; you're a bladdy overtight Hilux suspension spring about to snap."

There was a reason Jakkals had always been a leader to others. Always would be, no matter where he found himself.

43

The cowboy hat and Wrangler denim jacket and jeans still didn't match the picture Truter had conjured earlier in the interrogation room – a *Men in Black* agent wearing sunglasses indoors and a wire dangling from his ear. Instead, Pretoria had sent John Wayne to do their dirty work. Not that this made him any less uneasy about the SCU agent's unannounced arrival.

His feet and Stetson on the desk, his coffee mug empty, Captain Johan Engelbrecht tilted back in Truter's chair. "I'll say one thing for your deputy here. He makes a damn fine cuppa."

"How about another one, sir?"

"I'm good." Engelbrecht dropped the chair forwards and pushed the mug and untouched plate of Lemon Creams to the side. "What also impresses me here, Sergeant, is seeing your deputy taking detailed notes."

"If it's not on paper it might as well not exist, is what I tell my staff."

"Wise words, my friend." Engelbrecht drummed his fingers on the desk. "Right, gentlemen, fire away. I'm sure you have tons of questions."

Delport flipped back through his notebook. "If you don't mind, Captain, I do have a few," he said nervously. "There are some parts where I'm a bit confused."

"What's there to be confused about?" said Truter, eyeing

the Lemon Creams.

"Go for it, Constable. Like I already said, this thing's complicated."

"Thank you, sir. My first question then is, how long has this been going on for?"

"Hard to say, but from what we've stitched together so far, minimum three years, maybe four. It was only end of last year that the life insurance companies sniffed a rat."

Delport looked up from his notes. "If I am understanding this right, the big life insurance companies, Santam, Momentum, Liberty Life, these big companies underwrite ... Is that the right word?"

"Correct."

"So these big companies underwrite the small independent insurance brokers when there's a claim?"

"Yebo."

"And these small guys are then basically agents earning commission from the big companies for selling their life insurance products?"

"Exactly."

"But there must be hundreds of these small agents operating across the country?"

"More like thousands."

"*Easily* thousands, Delport," said Truter.

"And that's why it's so hard to track any fraud that might be going down?"

"You got it."

Delport turned back a page. "There's another thing I

don't quite understand—"

"Jissus, Delport, we don't have all day—"

"Your man is asking the right questions, Sergeant. Keep going."

"Thanks, sir. If I can then try sum it up, the process works like this …" Delport cleared his throat. "One. The insurance broker – that is, the agent – he sells a life insurance policy to Person A. Like you said earlier, someone who ticks the right boxes?"

"Ja, most of the time it's some whitey who doesn't qualify for full cover. Like your average middle-aged balie staring retirement in the face, who is now knuiping because he left his financial planning too late."

Delport pressed on. "Two. To make an easy sale, the broker will offer Person A a deal he can't refuse?"

"That's right. And let me tell you something: you'd also snap up the offer if you were in Person A's shoes. Because, just picture it … This gift horse comes knocking on your door, a respectable guy in a fancy suit and a fancy business card. Next thing, he's offering you life cover with Momentum, or some other posh company, at an unbelievable discount. Not only that, he'll make a few calls on the spot and sort out all the paperwork so you qualify for Comprehensive. Which idiot is going to say no to that?"

"What do you mean by 'sorting out the paperwork', Captain?"

"For starters, pumping up your non-existent income to

high earner status. Or magically getting rid of your so-called pre-existing health conditions. Emphysema? High blood pressure? Diabetes? No problem, sir, we'll take care of it. By the time the old balie has filled in the form, you'd swear he's Hussain bladdy Bolt."

Delport sucked on his pen. "Wow, sir, I see now what you mean by them making it easy." He flipped the page. "Three. You said that when someone signs up for full cover, they also get a package of free benefits to go with it. What would these be?"

"Okay, so not only will your family be left smiling when you kick the bucket, but from the day you sign up you accumulate loyalty points for all sorts of prizes."

"Like what?"

"Cellphones and airtime, fancy pens, bottles of whisky, pot-and-pan sets, holidays to Sun City, you name it. Too good to be true, hey?" Engelbrecht tilted back in the chair, allowing the police officers a breather. "That's because it is."

A field of frown lines had appeared across Delport's forehead. "I think I understand it to this point, sir, but now I'm lost again. You said the broking agent subsidises the life insurance policy. Are you saying they help pay the client's monthly premium, because that doesn't make—"

"That's exactly what I'm saying."

Truter nodded vehemently alongside Delport.

"But ... But if they're subsidising the life cover premiums and handing out all those free benefits, what's in it for them? Sorry, Captain, but I'm not getting it."

"No worries – this thing also took us time to unpick. Let's go through it again. On the surface, everything's hunky-dory. The client signs on the dotted line and is happy as Larry because he's just scored himself full life cover, with a funeral plan and a bunch of other perks thrown in for nothing. The boytjie is so happy he doesn't bother with the small print, the part about the insurance company becoming an investment partner. Even if he does read it, 'investment partner' sounds quite smart. And anyway, it's only fair the company gets their share for helping him pay his premiums." Engelbrecht stopped. "You're still looking confused, Constable. What about you, Sergeant?"

"Hundreds my side, Captain. All clear as day."

"Sir, I must be dof, because I still can't see how it makes financial sense."

"Okay, let me try explain it another way … Think of it like buying a Nando's share on the Johannesburg Stock Exchange. Except here you are buying a share in somebody's life insurance policy. What's more, you are not just buying a share in one person's policy, but in a whole bunch of policies. This company is invested in hundreds, even thousands of insurance policies."

"But surely that can't be legal, Captain?"

"Actually, it is. It happens all the time, especially in America."

"Makes perfect sense to me," said Truter, looking altogether more relaxed now that the immediate threat of arrest had passed. "All clear your side, Delport?"

"It's just—"

"In that case, how about we stop interrupting the captain for just one minute and let him finish?"

"I apologise, sir. It's just—"

"It's just what?" Truter lifted his hands in surrender. "I'm sorry for this, Captain—"

"It's just I don't understand how it can be a good investment for the insurance broking company," Delport blurted.

"What the hell is there not to understand?" hissed Truter. "One plus two equals three! Don't you get it?" This was fast approaching insubordination.

Engelbrecht stepped back to the sidelines. A smile had appeared at the corner of his mouth.

"What I mean is, if the investment partner company has to wait for the person to die before getting paid out, won't that take forever? Sorry, Captain, I must be missing something here?"

"I'll tell you what you're missing, Delport. A bag of bladdy marbles, that's what. I'm telling you, this—"

Engelbrecht lifted his hand to the air, halting Truter mid-flight like a miggie connecting the windscreen of the Joburg-to-Durban Intercity bus. "That's enough, Sergeant. Your deputy is one inch away from making the critical connection. I want you boys to understand this. Yes, you're spot on target, Constable. Who is going to wait fifteen, twenty, twenty-five years to get their money back on an investment? Hell, even the South African Post Office pays out quicker than that."

44

The Honourable Mayor Jakkals Dawid Venter stepped onto the makeshift stage. For the occasion he had chosen a blue Insignia pinstripe suit, a black shirt from Markham's (open at the collar), and brown Hushpuppies with beige socks. His greying hair was combed back, his moustache trimmed. Coupled with the gold mayoral chain, he exuded certain presidential status – albeit Banana Republic.

Jakkals walked up to the microphone and surveyed the small North West crowd assembling below – comprising the usual sunburnt faces dressed in Agri khaki, and women in those Sunday florals his wife liked to wear, that made them all look old before their time. Across the way, in front of the Bavaria Beer Tent, Freddie and Connie and that chop, Flip Vlok – who still owed him on the Nissan Skyline – were already hitting the Blackies. Not what he meant when he told them to have a good time.

Jakkals gazed up at the sky. Threatening clouds were building in the west. Closer to earth, behind the Insignia polyester, his itch was stirring into life; he still hadn't got around to buying his Mycota top-up.

He tapped the microphone. "Testing. Testing. Een,

twee, drie."

"Ons kan jou hoor, ou maat!" a voice shouted from the back.

"Dankie, meneer." Jakkals dug into his jacket pocket and unfolded the A4. What with all the operational crap going down, he'd left his speech to the last minute. Swallowing back a lump of phlegm, he cleared his throat. It was time to get the show on the road.

"Ladies and gentleman. Dames en here. As mayor of Brits, I most heartily welcome you all here today, to this, the fifth North West Southern Districts Agri Festival." A small cheer floated off the crowd, the bulk of it emanating from the beer tent. "Thank you. Dankie. It's a very exciting day for our region, which could not happen without the efforts of many hard-working people. You can all give yourselves a slap on the back for achieving what you have achieved." Jakkals glanced down at his bullet points. "If I just look around me, it's fantastic to see what can be done when people decide to pull together. Gesaamheid – spelt with a capital G!" He cleared his throat. "With so many brilliant stalls and exciting events happening through the day, I hardly know where to begin." A kid had started whining to the far left of him – hundred bucks on the table it was Ryan. He pressed on. "For example, how about starting your afternoon at the international food stall? That is one table I will be visiting, because I hear the American waffles are something out of this world. A big thank you to the church committee for making that one possible. Excellent job, ladies." An appreciative twitter rippled through his audience. He cleared his throat. "Then of course, we all look forward to the main event of the day, the Potjie Play-off. A huge thumbs-up to the guys at Edendal Agri for hosting this year. Where are you? Okay, I see you there at the back. Let's give the Agri guys a big hand of applause, ladies and gentlemen … From what I hear, the competition is as stiff as a Hilux spring this year." More laughter – his speech was going down well. "In fact, I can already see the steam rising from our contestants standing at the ready by their fires. So, all I can say is good luck to all of you mense." Jakkals scanned the A4. Below it, his rash was screaming out for a good and proper scratch. "What makes this year's play-off even more special is that we are honoured to have Northern Free State champion Nils Botha as one of our judges. Thank you, Nils, for travelling all this way." He gazed over towards the beer tent. Where the hell had Freddie and them got to? This was no time to get pissed. "On a day like today, ladies and gentlemen, we must stop and reflect on how blessed we are, because we have many things to be thankful for. Just look at what's going down in America and Europe … ISIS terrorists chopping people's heads off, the Muslims and Corolla virus invading all over the place, the overpopulation problems, global heating, the Brexit." Jakkals pointed an accusing finger at the heavens. "The pollution is so bad in Europe, you can't see the sky any more! My brother-in-law in England tells me people are living on top of one another like rats in tiny cages, mense." Jakkals was now speaking off-script. "Half the kids have never seen a wild animal. They don't even know where milk comes from. Kan julle dit glo?" Jakkals waited for the laughter to subside. "So then, kom ons bid and give thanks for what we have … Dankie, Here, thank you, Lord, for blessing the people of South Africa, for sharing with us your wonderful bounties. For the blue sky, for the clean flowing rivers, for the fertile land in which we plant our wheat, for the high mountains, for the animals that roam freely across the plains. Dankie vir alles, liewe Here. Amen!" Jakkals opened his eyes.

People were starting to look at their watches. The whining brat to the left had started up again – it sounded just like Ryan. A solid dose of Ritlon – or whatever they called the stuff – that would sort him out chop-chop. It was time to wrap up. "Ladies and gentlemen, I hereby declare this year's Agri Festival officially open! Thank you! Dankie! And enjoy yourselves!" And with that, Jakkals Venter stepped off the stage, jammed his hand into his trouser pocket and gave his crotch a desperately overdue claw.

45

"So, what you're saying, Captain, the life insurance payouts are happening quicker than before?"

"Way quicker, my friend. Based on what we've worked out so far, we're now looking at less than two years from sign up to sign out."

Delport was spellbound. "Less than two years! And you discovered this from analysing the stats of the big insurance companies?"

"Yebo. Santam, Momentum, and a couple of other big boys. And of course the stats you guys and the other stations have been supplying for the past few months. Which we thank you for, by the way."

His eyes glowing, Delport turned to his boss. "Didn't I say there was something going on, Sergeant?"

"Ja, ja, Delport, don't wet yourself now."

"I'm just saying, sir—"

"Thank you, Delport, but I think the captain would like to move on. Not so, Captain?"

"No rush. You were about to ask something else, Constable?"

"Yes, sir." Delport ran a finger down the page of his notebook. "Oh, yes. How many victims are we talking so far?"

"Moerse hard to tell, because most of them would already be dead and buried. Remember, this thing's been going on for a few years, but the insurance companies only sniffed a rat last year. We can't exactly start digging up bodies across the country just because someone had a life insurance policy, can we now? And even if we did, we wouldn't find anything."

"I understand, sir. So it was only when you started analysing the stats that this company's figures stuck out from all the rest?"

"Like a sore thumb with an ingrown nail. But we still had to drill in deep to see the pattern."

"How long is the average insurance payout supposed to be?"

Truter shook his head in amazement. Delport was an embarrassment to the force, butting in with all these ridiculous questions.

"More like twenty or thirty years. What's fascinating is watching the turnaround from this lot getting shorter all the time." Engelbrecht shifted his gaze to Truter. "Which means what, Sergeant?"

"Your guess is as good as mine, Captain."

"It means they're getting greedy, or seriously cocky … Or both."

"Incredible," said Truter. At this point, he was looking increasingly like a tourist who had lost his way in a foreign city.

"Something more, Constable?"

"Just going back a step here, sir, what about the death certificates and those reports we've been filling in for Pretoria? Wouldn't the cause of death show that a victim died in suspicious circumstances?"

"If only it was so easy, my friend. But no, with a bag of tricks from their Special Ops days, this lot is super clever; they know how to cover their tracks. Every suspected victim we've identified so far has died from so-called 'natural causes'. We're also now convinced they have a medical specialist working for them on the inside, rigging the death certificates and other covert shenanigans."

"Like what natural causes?"

"Asthma attacks, heart and liver failures, pedestrian accidents – plenty of those – boozing it up and drowning in the swimming pool, slipping in the bath, food poisoning, that type of thing. We even have a suspected victim who died from choking on a drive-through KFC chicken bone. But so far not one suicide. Because why?"

"I don't know, sir"

"Because the big life insurers don't cover suicide ... Something wrong, Sergeant?"

"No, all hundreds."

"You sure? Maybe it was my mention of Special Ops?"

"Is this who these people are, sir? Special Ops?"

"According to our background checks, ja. Just a sec, Delport ... If I'm right, Sergeant, didn't you serve active duty in 22-Battalion?"

Truter stared up at the ceiling, avoiding the SCU agent's penetrating gaze. "Ag, maybe years ago."

"For which you received a Medal of Honour. Am I right?"

"Jeez, Sergeant, I didn't know that."

"It's no big deal, Delport."

"And if I have my facts straight, you then served two years as a security operative at The Farm. Is that correct?"

"Wow, you didn't tell me any of this stuff, sir. Was that before you were promoted to Benoni Dog Unit?"

"Didn't you hear me, Delport? I said it's no big deal."

"Sorry, sir, I'm just interested."

"Well, go be interested somewhere else."

Engelbrecht knew he had hit a nerve; he'd been right all along. From what he had worked out from Truter's case file, the transfer to Dog Unit was the turning point. It didn't take a State-employed shrink to know damaged goods when it was staring him in the face; any idiot could do that. But the report told only half the story. *Severe post-traumatic stress disorder, with resultant paranoid tendencies. The patient has been exposed to multiple events of a violent nature while serving active duty in Angola.* Blah, blah. The 'multiple events of a violent nature' had bugger-all to do with it – after all, the guy was a natural-born soldier. The real reason for his downwards spiral was good old-fashioned betrayal. Triggered the day his trusted military brothers tossed him to the wolves – first De Klerk's internal enquirers into the murder and mayhem that went down on The Farm, followed by the pussyfooting TRC. Now that Engelbrecht could see first-hand the knife of Brutus sticking out from Truter's back, it was clear as day: no chance in hell he had anything to do with this dirty tricks bunch.

"If you don't mind, Sergeant, I'd like you to help me with a few names here. Maybe you've heard of them. Okay with that? ... Great stuff. Okay, the first one ...

Frederick Ferreira?"

Truter nodded blankly. "Served with him."

"Juan Dippenaar? Otherwise known as Dippies."

"Same. Served with him."

"Byl Minnaar?"

"Ja."

"Rudolph Scheepers? AKA Choppies."

"Worked sometimes with him at VIP Protection Agency."

"Conrad Botes? Or shall I say Dr Conrad Botes?"

"22-Battalion medic."

Engelbrecht gave the knife a final twist. "Jakkals Venter?"

Truter nodded, his face still blank. But Engelbrecht could see what was going down behind the eyes. "He was our commanding officer."

"22-Battalion?"

"Ja.

"And The Farm?"

"Ja."

"Thank you, Sergeant. I appreciate it," said Engelbrecht gently. He shut his notebook. "The list goes on, gentlemen." The mood in the room had turned sombre. "I suppose you want to know what the connection is, Constable?"

"Only if it's okay with you."

"What we have here, gents, is a group of ex-military who've made the successful shift into the big bucks of the private death industry. These names, each and every one of them is today a director or employee of Titanium Financial Services." Engelbrecht allowed a moment, then slapped his notebook on the desk. "You know what, Constable?"

"Yes, sir?"

"I think we can all do with another cup of your lekker coffee. What you say, Sergeant Truter?"

Truter smiled weakly. "That will be good. Three sugars, Delport."

"No problem." Delport stood up and quickly gathered the empty mugs. He paused at the door. "I was just wondering, Captain ..."

"Wondering what?"

"About the thing you said earlier about there not being enough hard evidence to pin on these guys. Why is that?"

Engelbrecht stared hard at the water stain on the ceiling, not wanting to confront a bitter truth. "Because, Delport, all we've got so far is stats, stats, and more bladdy stats. According to the big shot State lawyers we can't make any arrests, because in their book the evidence is so-called circumstantial. How messed up is that, hey?" Engelbrecht shaped a ring between his thumb and index finger, leaving a tiny gap between the two. "This is how close we are, manne ... but still no fokken cigar."

46

Far bigger than the sum of its parts, the Edendal Potjie Play-off was the backbone of the local cultural calendar. Less one-off event than complex ritual – of unspoken codes of conduct, behind-the-scenes pacts, and jealously guarded recipes – it simmered for months before coming to a fast boil on the day. Few escaped its grip: one was either direct participant or participant by association. There was no middle ground, no fence-sitting.

Tensions were now running high under a blue haze of smoke and burnt boerewors at the far end of the Agricultural Showgrounds. Squeezed between the ablution block and a ginger-haired braai veteran in black rugby shorts and a gut sponsored by Kempton Park Isuzu, Steve and Tarryn Aldridge stood behind their fold-out camping table, anxiously awaiting the judges. The stand was a picture of military precision: the potjie polished to a high gleam, with the contents simmering quietly under the lid; below, a neatly arranged circle of glowing coals; to the side, the tools of their craft hanging on a purpose-built rack. The Jurgens' tablecloth covered the camping table. Concealed under it, the cooler box.

"Stevie, how about I get you a nice beer to relax?"

"Maybe I should have one. I'm jittery as anything."

"Don't be, we're almost there. Just a few more hours and I promise you, we're home dry."

"I don't know if I can last a few more hours," croaked Aldridge, looking over towards the ginger-hair gent. "Seriously, I feel like I'm going to have a nervous breakdown. I can't take the tension any more."

"I also feel like that, but we've just got to bite the bullet and finish what we've started. What's the time now?"

"Just after two-thirty."

"And the judging starts when?

"Three. At least, that's what they said."

"Which means … by four o' clock, it's all over, babes!"

Aldridge glanced nervously around him. "Geez, not so loud, Tarryn. The guy might hear you."

"Sorry. I'm just excited we're so close to putting this whole thing behind us."

"I keep telling myself the same thing. It's the only thing keeping me going right now."

"Have you heard from the garage yet?"

Aldridge dropped to his haunches and shifted the coals around.

"Do you really need to keep doing that?"

"Sorry, just trying to stay busy. I did."

"Did what?"

"Hear from them."

"And?"

Aldridge stood up and pushed back on his aching hips. "They said the car will be ready this afternoon."

"Crikey, Stevie, why didn't you tell me? Are you serious?"

"I was going to tell you, but first wanted to make

hundred per cent sure."

"That's fantastic news, babes!"

"Seriously, Tarryn, not so loud!"

"Sorry. But who here cares, anyway?"

"You never know—"

"So we can collect it straight after we've packed up here?"

"I guess."

"And be on the road by this evening? Like, actually drive away from this hell hole in our own car?"

"That's the plan."

Tarryn gazed up at the sky, at the bank of dark cloud in the distance. "I can't believe it."

"Tell me about it."

"You're smiling, Steve. For the first time in days, you're actually smiling."

"Sorry, I'll try not to if you want. So are you, by the way."

Tarryn squeezed her husband's hand. Looked him deep in the eyes. "I think I'm going to cry ... From relief ... And happiness."

"We better not get too excited. I'll only believe it when we're sitting behind the wheel."

"This definitely deserves a drink."

"I reckon so. You want me to fetch?"

"No, I'll go. I need a pee, anyway."

"You don't want to take a quick look first?"

"I didn't dare ask."

"You had better … just in case … Careful, the lid's hot. Maybe use this cloth."

Tarryn Aldridge cautiously lifted the potjie lid, releasing a sweet steamy bouquet of onion, garlic, rosemary, Old Brown Sherry and tender lamb. "It smells good, Steve. There's no ways…" She peered through the steam. "Pass me that big spoon … Thanks." Carefully stirring the contents, Tarryn separated out the cubes of meat from the thick sauce and the carrots and potatoes.

"What you think?" Aldridge whispered anxiously from behind her.

"There is no ways, Steve. If I didn't know better—"

"You not just saying so?"

"No. Even the smell … How much is left in the Coleman?"

"Nothing."

"You mean this is all of it?"

"Besides, you know … and what we fed to the dog and all."

Tarryn replaced the lid and gazed up at her husband. Her eyes were filled with wonder and new-found respect. "It's all in here? Every last bit is in this pot …"

"Except, you know…"

"Apart from that."

"Yes, every last bit is in there."

She climbed unsteadily to her feet. "I need a pee. And I need a Brutal Fruit. I need a seriously cold Brutal Fruit."

47

Giving the room a final sweep, Johan Engelbrecht pulled the door shut behind him. Buffalo had done the job, but he wouldn't be running back any day soon. He still hadn't figured out his next move – drive back to Pretoria for the weekend, or sit it out and see what came up? On either count he had to keep moving. He had to keep the leads flowing.

He contemplated giving Cynthia a quick call, then shoved the thought aside; she would have called by now if she had something for him. Besides, he'd given her enough to work with. The woman could only do what the woman could do.

He decided he would toss a coin later, to head back to Pretoria or not. Until then he could kill the afternoon with a visit to another mortuary – collect more names for Cynthia to run background checks on. There was no telling what might come up – that New Horizons dump was proof of it. He could tick off that box, head home for the weekend if he felt like it, and be back again in the area by Monday lunchtime. Any plan was better than staring a weekend alone in the magoelas.

But first things first: pay the bill and blow this joint.

He headed down the side of the house, following the laminated arrows to Reception Office. He knocked on the sliding door. Knocked again. Cupping his hands, he peered through the mesh curtain. Nada. He would leave the cash on the desk. He pulled on the door. Music was coming from down the passage. Opera. First problem of the day: he had no idea what he owed. He stepped into the passage. The music was coming from three doors down. A bedroom. This was fast getting messier than a cash-in-transit heist gone wrong.

He tapped softly on the door. For some unknown reason, his heart was beating faster than its usual fifty-four BPM. He leant in against the door – a woman's voice, singing along with the music. The voice wasn't half bad. Something primal stirred deep in his gut.

Engelbrecht lifted his hand to knock again, hesitated, resisting the unknown. The something primal had shown its face: raw, careless yearning. He stared at the door. This was asking for trouble. Spelt with a capital "T". He clamped down on his jaw as he watched the hand take hold of the handle, as if controlled by an outside force – the careless yearning was fast getting the better of him.

He now saw it for what it was, the electric static he'd felt pass between them. Standing there under the light the night before, then again when he had gone in to ask for fresh milk for his coffee. Engelbrecht was no stranger to loneliness and also knew longing when he saw it. She *had* to have felt it too.

Fokkit! He had been down this road one time too many – breaking up with the ex hadn't even formed a scab, and here he was asking for more of the same. Pulling himself to himself, he had made up his mind. No silly buggers. No mixing business with pleasure. Hand over the cash. Say goodbye. Walk away. Don't look back.

Engelbrecht pressed down on the handle.

Susan Meissner was swaying gently in front of the bedroom mirror, her eyes closed. Soft silvery light filtered through the curtains. She was barefoot, her hair down, wearing a red dress that stopped above her knees. Engelbrecht stood anchored to the floor, mouth dry. Retreat was out of the question – she had already sixth-sensed his presence. Slowing mid-sway, eyes opening, face already turning pink, hand lifting towards mouth in embarrassment.

"Oh, God, I thought everyone was out … This is so—"

"Sorry, it's my fault. I should have knocked louder. I didn't realise you were—"

"I feel so ridiculous."

"You think you feel ridiculous? Look at me standing here like an idiot for barging in on you." Engelbrecht laughed. "Maybe we must change the subject. What you say?"

"Yes, maybe that's a good idea." Her hands dropped to her side.

"I like this music. What is it?"

"Puccini."

"It's nice. It matches your dress. What I mean is—"

"I'll try take that as a compliment." She was now smiling shyly. No longer blushing.

"It's a beautiful dress." He meant it.

"This old thing? It's just a—

"What with this nice music and the light through the curtain, I swear, you look like a flipping film star."

The words had come out clumsy and cheesy. But he meant them – the bashful and beautiful woman standing in front of him did look like a flipping film star. He could have told her the same thing the night before when she was wearing that kimono number.

Susan Meissner tossed back her long brown hair and laughed. An open honest laugh. "Nobody's said that to me before. Not even my husband … Especially not my husband."

"Well, maybe he should, because it's true."

"It is?"

"Yes, hundred and ten per cent."

"That's … I don't know how I should take it—"

Engelbrecht's phone was ringing in his pocket. "Shit, sorry—"

"Shouldn't you answer it?"

"Ja, I suppose I better." He wrestled the Samsung out of his jean's pocket – maybe it was Cynthia with news. "SAPS Edendal" flashed back at him. What the hell did *they* want? But whatever it was, they could wait. He pressed down on the power button and shoved the phone back into his pocket. Any remaining shards of rational thought were now fast dissolving. He looked up to meet her penetrating gaze. Her eyes were on fire, her lips red and moist.

48

Aldridge's hand trembled as he lifted the potjie lid and ladled the sauce over Otto's Meissner's paper plate.

"Let me help you there, sweetie ... Looks like the nerves have got to my husband. Mr Venter, would you also like some more yummy sauce?"

Jakkals Venter held out his plate. "If not, why not? It smells damn tasty."

"And how about you, Mr Botha?"

"I'm good. Got to save myself."

"I see you could definitely do with a meat top-up, Mr Meissner?"

"Come on, girlie, none of this Mr Meissner. For you, it's Otto."

Tarryn smiled coyly. "Sorry, I mean Otto." She nudged her husband with her elbow. "Steve, the man's hungry."

"Did I say, or did I not say you people would have a good time in our little town?" Licking his lips, Meissner inched closer to Tarryn. "You know what our motto is?"

"Where you arrive a stranger and leave a friend?"

"Exactamont!" Meissner closed his eyes. "This now smells good. What you think, Nils? Are our friends from Sasolburg in for a chance?"

Nils Botha prodded the chunks of meat on his plate. "So far, so good. I'm impressed by how soft and tender this lamb is. You see how it's falling off the bone here, gents? That's one of the things you must look for as a judge. The meat must be just right. Not tough like an old tyre, but also not boiled to death." Botha set his plate down on the fold-up table, retrieved the pencil from behind his ear, and scribbled a note on his scorecard. Taking their cue, Meissner and Venter followed suit. "I won't ask where you people get your lamb, but this is quality. Definitely not Shoprite."

Venter shovelled a forkful of meat into his mouth and swallowed hungrily. "Bladdy tasty, that's all I'll say."

"And I'll eat to that," said Meissner. "Check how nervous these people are. You would swear we are in the Olympic Games."

The Free State champion gave his plate another prod. "And I like what you've done here with the sauce. The sweet of the dried fruit and OBS isn't so hectic that it drowns out the taste of the meat. A big mistake we often come across in judging."

"Thanks, Mr Botha. We actually used a different sherry for this recipe. A more expensive one that's less sweet. Isn't that right, Steve?"

Mesmerised by the simmering potjie, Aldridge looked up and smiled weakly. "Yes, it's a less sweet one."

"Nice. Very nice." Botha turned to his co-judges. "I will say these city slickers know what they're doing."

Meissner had scraped his plate clean, and for a man of limited stature had a surprisingly large appetite. "What was that herby thingie going on in there?"

"It's called rosemary, Mr— Otto. How about a last scoop for you?"

"Hold your horses, boys. We're not even halfway down the line yet."

Meissner shrugged. "Sorry, but you heard the man, girlie. I have to say no."

"Of course, I understand," said Tarryn, sending another coy smile the wolf's way. "In that case, how about a tot of sherry before you hardworking men move on?"

"Tarryn, I don't think they—"

"Nice touch, people. Matching the potjie with a sherry tasting. Very clever." Nils Botha scribbled on his scorecard.

"I won't say no to a quick sherry … cherry."

Tarryn giggled. "That's really funny, Otto. Don't you think so, Steve?"

Aldridge forced yet another weak smile. "Definitely."

As if suddenly remembering something of great import, Meissner pulled back his sleeve and checked his watch.

"Something wrong, Otto?"

"Wrong? Oh no! Definitely nothing wrong. I'm expecting a very important business call," he said smugly. "Concerning a big investment deal, if you must know. Tight deadlines. Big game pressure—"

"Wow. A man of many talents."

"Yes, girlie, you could say that."

"Okay, gents, down the hatch and then we must keep moving, because we still have three contestants to go." Nils Botha tilted his bush hat at the couple. "Nice one, people. I'm impressed. You can now open up to the public."

Meissner threw back the contents of his paper cup, wiped

his chin, and gave Tarryn a final look-in. "See you later, alligator."

"In a while, crocodile."

The couple watched the man scuttle after the other two judges. Tarryn turned to her husband.

"Socks and Crocs. Can you actually believe it?"

49

"What we drinking this time, Constable?"

"Nescafe Gold, sir."

"You boys don't mess around."

Truter fired a caustic look Delport's way. "The station only has it on special occasions, Captain. The rest of the time we drink Ricoffy. Not so, Delport?"

"Don't look so worried, man. You can drink fancy filter coffee for all I care. We all work hard for a living and deserve a treat now and then. Anyways, back to business. Delport, you left a message on my cell that you had something important to show me? So here I am, gents, at your disposal. Sergeant, any idea what this is about?"

Truter shrugged his shoulders. "Don't look at me. I hope you're not planning to waste our time, Delport, because some of us have important work to do."

"I understand, sir." Delport opened his blue folder. His hands were shaking. "Sergeant, you know the USB stick you asked me to take a look at?"

Truter coughed. "This is not the time or place—"

"Well, I managed to open it on my computer and I found—"

"Didn't you hear me, man? I said this is not—"

"Jissus, give the guy a chance, Truter."

"I'm just saying, Captain—"

"There were some files that I think you might find interesting, sir."

"Is that them there? Looks like a heap."

"Yes, sir. I printed them all out, so I could study them at home."

"I'm still clueless where this is going, but carry on, boet."

Truter bent down and proceeded to extricate a syringa berry from the underside of his boot. "I rest my case."

"So, um, basically, these printouts are all Excel spreadsheets," said Delport. He tentatively inched the stapled ream in the SCU agent's direction. "As you can see, it's mostly just columns of codes and numbers."

"Yes, I can see that. Lots of codes and numbers."

"It took me a while, but I think I know what they are."

"I also think I know what they are," said Truter, flicking the berry to the floor. "Gobbledygook. Jesus, Delport, I'm just about up to here!"

"Truter! Zip it. Alright, let me take a squizz." Engelbrecht adjusted his reading glasses. "'Client Ref, Co Ref, Date 1, Date 2, S/total 1, S/total 2, Nett.' Can't say these headers mean anything to me."

"For example, sir, the numbers under Client Ref got me thinking that maybe they were identity numbers of people. So, just for fun I ran—"

Truter rolled his head in disbelief. "'Just for fun.' You hear that, Captain?"

"What I mean is, I decided to run some of the numbers through the system to see if anything would come up."

"And? Did anything come up?"

"Yes, sir. They are identity numbers of actual people." Delport reached nervously into the blue folder and pulled out another page. "These are the names the system came up with."

"Okay, lemme see."

"Why's your hand shaking, Delport?"

"I'm not sure why, Sergeant."

Engelbrecht was now sitting more upright. "Is this all of them?"

"No, just the first page, sir. But I can easily check the rest."

For a few moments silence descended over Truter's office. Broken by a long slow whistle. "If this is what I think it is … Where did you say these files came from again?"

"The USB stick that—"

"Oh, ja, the USB stick. Can I borrow your pen, Constable?"

"Sure, sir."

The muscles of his jaw working hard, Engelbrecht ran a finger down the page, popping off the names as he went. "John Simmonds. Tick! Adrian Daniels. Tick! Gerald Phelps. Nope. Hans de Bruyn, Tick! Roger Henley. Tick! John Andrews. Nope. Jerry Conradie. Nope. Gary Johnson. Nope. Phillip van der Spuy. Tick!" Engelbrecht looked up from the page, his eyes now glowing like some nocturnal predator. "Keep talking, my friend. You have my full attention."

"All deceased, sir."

"Who all deceased?"

"The names you marked with ticks. They're all recently deceased."

"Now you've got me. How the hell do you know that?"

"Because I cross-checked."

A Wimbledon spectator watching a Nadal-Federer rally, Truter's eyes darted back and forth between the SCU agent and his deputy. Simultaneously, something in the deeper recesses of his brain was worming its way towards the light. "Roger Henley and Gary Johnson? How come I know those bladdy names …"

Delport was struggling to contain himself. "That's what got me interested, Sergeant, because I instantly recognised them when I ran the ID numbers through the SAPS database. Gary Johnson is the missing person we've been looking for. And Henley is the guy from North West Motor Spares who died the other day."

"Take it slow, Constable. Did you say missing person?"

Delport breathed in deeply. Counted to five. "Yes, Captain. His girlfriend reported him missing two days ago. He disappeared while taking a morning jog."

"Now, that is interesting."

"Captain, do you want to know what else I worked out from the spreadsheet?"

"What, you have more?"

"Lots more. I know what 'Co Ref' stands for: Company Reference. The codes you see under that header are short for the names of big insurance companies. 'OM' stands for Old Mutual, 'STM' for Santam, 'LL' for Liberty Life, 'MTM' for Momentum."

Engelbrecht studied the page. "You know what, I think you're right … Unfokkenbelievable."

"'Date 1' is when the person signed up with the life insurance company."

"And 'Date 2'?"

"Date 2 is when the person died; I've already cross-checked some of them, and the information matches what we have on the SAPS database."

"Incredible … And what about these blank spaces?"

"Easy, sir. Those are people that aren't dead yet."

His head still rocking from side to side in amazement, Engelbrecht sat back and contemplated the freckly carrot top on the far side of the desk. How he'd ended up in the arse end of the world alongside the likes of Bossies Truter was beyond him. There had to be others just like him: undiscovered diamonds buried in the dust. The system was fucked. "I don't know what to say. I seriously don't know. It's like someone's crept up from behind and moered me on the back of the head with a panga. With this information …" Engelbrecht's brain was racing ahead of itself, working through the legal and practical implications. One tiny unanswered question remained. A question he would have preferred to ignore. "Sorry, menere, but I have to ask you now, where did the USB stick come from? And, listen, I don't need to hear all the gory details, just where it came from. Sergeant?"

Truter looked at Delport. Delport looked back at Truter.

"Yes, Sergeant? We're waiting."

Truter followed the SCU agent's gaze to the water leak on the ceiling, then down again to the desk. "Ag, it's no big deal, Captain," he said as casually as was possible in the circumstances. "It was in the drawer of Jakkals Venter's office."

Engelbrecht let out a long slow controlled whistle. "Fok my dood!"

50

Otto Meissner was no longer feeling so chipper, now that the effects of the Blood River Artisan Ale were wearing thin, combined with the worrying fact that the Galactic

Tours rep hadn't called from the bank like he promised he would. His earlier euphoria had given way to a gnawing tapeworm.

His bunch of master keys dangling at his side, Meissner poked his head into the passage – all clear. He tiptoed down the corridor and halted in front of Rhino Room and pressed his ear against the door. Slipping the master key into the lock, he opened the door quietly, stepped inside, and locked it behind him.

The curtains were still drawn; the dank air hung heavy with male BO and mature Brie. He groped for the light switch and waited for the fluorescent tube to flicker into life. As it did so, the tapeworm in his gut took another large bite: the man's clothing was strewn across the floor; a pair of fire-engine red tanga briefs were stretched taut over the bedside lamp as a makeshift shade; balls of toilet paper lay heaped at the side of the bed. A beaten-to-death leather suitcase with stickers and straps gaped open on the bed.

Navigating gingerly through the debris, Meissner worked his way over to the pine wardrobe and pulled on the handle – empty. He pulled out the drawer below – ditto. Fending off the early stirrings of panic, he shifted his attention to the suitcase, approaching the task as one would a dog turd on the front doorstep. The contents included (in no particular order of importance): a blue-check toiletry bag with a broken zip containing a tube of roll-on Brut deodorant; a crusty tortoise-shell comb; a tub of Vaseline;

a gummed-up razor blade; earbuds in various shades of yellow; a half-bar of Lux soap wrapped in Jiffy. Shoved in below, a pair of beige Stokies; a faux snakeskin belt; a white vest; a knotted plastic bag with Wimpy sugar, Cremora and Ricoffy sachets; a BIC lighter; two pairs of black socks; a blue Insignia tie; a pair of Markham underpants with a stain on the crotch; an Okapi penknife; and various loose cash receipts.

Meissner pulled hard on his goatee, forcing rounded rationality into a square hole – things were not always what they seemed to be; there *had* to be an explanation, although his pounding temples and powder-dry lips were telling him otherwise. He repacked the suitcase contents, dropped to his haunches and peered under the bed – other than a crusty sock, the search came up empty. He stood up, his back now aching, and walked over to the window and tore open the curtain. He stared into the dying afternoon, barely registering his wife's questioning look from the washing line.

Blinking hard, repeating to himself there had to be a good explanation to all this, Otto Meissner turned back to the room. Only now did he notice the green Anorak on the chair. One of those jackets that had been through the wars, what with the collar rubbed through and the elbow pad ripped. He tentatively squeezed the pockets, then flipped the jacket upside down and gave it a violent shake. Loose coins, a strapless Casio watch, a confetti of Peppermint wrappers, and a Medic Alert bracelet cascaded to the floor. Meissner hurled the Anorak across the room, before falling back into the chair in despair.

Abrahams, or whatever his name was, was good; he couldn't deny him that. He had swallowed the Galactic Tours story, hook, line, and sinker. The guy had eaten his food, drunk his whisky, slept in his bed, emptied his bar fridge, and by now cashed his ten thousand ront cheque. The only thing he hadn't done to him was fornicated with his wife. Meissner groaned, then reached limply for the bracelet. He turned it over, staring blankly at the faded lettering. He twisted it to the light, trying to make out the medical sob story. The jackhammering in his head was threatening to explode. Black spots floated back and forth across the room. He groped at his (empty) shirt pocket for his glasses—

Succumbing to a toxic mix of despair and rage, Otto Meissner hurled the Medic Alert against the bedroom far wall. For an ever-so-brief moment it hung suspended in mid-air, before disappearing from view behind the pine headboard.

51

A hand was tugging urgently at Tarryn Aldridge's sleeve.

"What's wrong?"

"There!"

"Where? What?"

"There, flipping hell, at the gate!"

Tarryn tracked her husband's stunned stare. "Oh, sweet Jesus, Stevie!" Even at a distance there was no mistaking *Him* – battering ram head dropped forwards, thighs apart, hand fingering holster, vacuum-packed biceps. Judging by the way the psycho cop was scanning the terrain, this was no social visit. What's more, he had come with backup – in the form of a skinny red-haired policeman. Tarryn bit hard into her lip, pushing down on a wave of fear that threatened to engulf and sweep her away. It was game over.

Cowering behind her, Aldridge was also watching his life unravel before him. They were everywhere – the SWAT team – disguised as civilians, fanning out in every direction, blocking off the exits, taking up position: one of them standing guard at the beer tent, dressed in khaki, another two in tracksuits and bush hats at the turnstiles. Reinforcements were streaming in through the gate, mingling with the crowd, their weapons and bullet-proof vests hidden under camo hunting jackets. His head felt hot: infrared crosshairs of police snipers trained on him from up on the spectator stands. But he had to be strong. Strong for Tarryn. Go quietly. Go like a man.

"We tried, Stevie. We really tried."

"I know. It's okay—"

"We did our best—"

"We did our best. It wasn't meant to be—"

Tarryn dug her nails into his arm. "He's seen us! Oh my

God, Steve, they're coming for us."

"Whatever you do, don't move," Aldridge whispered hoarsely. His brain had watched enough "Man Encounters Angry Mother Grizzly" videos on YouTube to override the fight-or-flight instinct, opting instead to play dead.

At the far side of the Agri Showgrounds arena, Truter was fast losing patience and gatvol of hanging around. "Come, Delport, it's time to make a move."

"But sir, mustn't we await our instructions from—"

"Fok that. I know how this lot from Pretoria operates. The cows will be home asleep by the time they get their poepols into gear. If we don't go now, we're gonna miss our chance. Kom ons gaan!"

Abandoning his post at Exit 1, Truter cut a path through the dawdling ice-cream lickers, trailed by a nervous Constable Delport. Engelbrecht's earlier strategy brief — that this was to be a clean operation with minimal loss to civilian life and limb – had long since flown Truter's coop, now that the opportunity to finally prove his mettle to God and country (and Pretoria, for that matter), had presented itself. He was intent on squeezing out every last drop.

Delport caught up with him. "Sir, you really don't think we should hold back? Oh, bliksem—" Stepping over the woman his boss had just knocked to the ground, he slalomed around her tray of disembowelled boerewors. "Sorry, mevrou, South African Police Services." People were now beginning to stare, sensing something was about to go down. Delport hurried on after his superior.

"Delport, you got me covered?" called Truter from the front.

Sucked along by the wake of raw animal power and passion, Delport threw aside his remaining misgivings. "Behind you all the way, sir!"

"That's my boy!" shouted Truter, and with that reached down and unleashed his .38 in an impressive flowing arc action – simultaneously triggering a seismic ripple of public panic. Women and children scattered before him, adult men scurried behind stall tables, popcorn was strewn across the ground like confetti at a wedding.

Drunk on a heady mix of bloodlust, boerewors, and the distant clatter of police chopper blades, Truter had passed the point of no return. He had waited twenty-five years for redemption and could now taste the revenge coming his way – a revenge sweeter than a home-baked koeksuster dipped in syrup. Nobody, but nobody was going to stand between him and delivering the fatal blow.

Coordinating (the just recently dubbed) "Operation Red Jackal" from high up on the spectator stand, Captain Johan Engelbrecht had been caught off-guard by the sudden turn of events unfolding below. Taking rapid stock of the situation, he knew he had a potential bloodbath on his hands – there would be hell to pay if civilian lives were lost. He lowered his binocs and chewed hard on the inside of his cheek, weighing up the options.

Including Bossies Truter in the operation – a decision motivated solely by pity – had been a gross error of judgement. Inferring from the singular intent of the animal weaving through the crowd below, it was already blatantly obvious they'd have an easier time stopping a charging bull rhino. Engelbrecht turned to the SCU ops member behind him.

"Pass me the radio, we'll try one more time … Sergeant Truter, come in!" No response. "Constable Delport, are you there?" Nothing. "Truter, I order you to pull back." Engelbrecht handed the radio back. "The psycho's gone rogue." He lifted his binocs and adjusted the focus ring. Extrapolating from Truter's due-north trajectory, his target had to be the grand Lotto prize – head honcho himself, Jakkals Venter.

Up until the moment Truter had gone walkabout, the SCU task team had been tracking Venter's movements and had him where they wanted him – wandering slowly in the direction of Exit 2 and the yellow Hummer, away from the crowds, because there was no way of knowing what these paranoid ex-Ops were packing, or for that matter what they were prepared to do to get out of a tight spot. A messy hostage situation was on the cards if they didn't get them out the area soon. Engelbrecht arced the binocs ninety degrees to the left and locked on Juan Dippenaar. His kid was on his shoulders, his wife trailing behind, making their way towards the car park and the midnight-black Navarra under the blue gums. Engelbrecht adjusted his focus. "I don't see Botes? Hans, you still got a fix on him?"

"Sitting vas like Loctite at eleven o' clock, approx three hundred metres."

"Okay, I got him." Conrad Botes appeared to be alone, a beer in his hand, stuffing his face with a boerewors roll. "What about Ferreira? Who the heck's tracking Ferreira?"

"Me, sir ... I had him until a few seconds ago ... Hang on, I see him again; just came out the bogs. Heading back in direction of beer tent."

"All right, good. Make sure you don't lose him."

"Roger that!"

Engelbrecht raked his binoculars back and forth across the main showground arena. Where the hell had he got to?

"Please tell me one of you have a lock on Venter. Denzel?"

"Negative, Captain. He went behind the food stalls and hasn't come out yet. Maybe he's gone out the back entrance?"

"I don't need to hear maybes. Come on, manne, this is *not* the time to drop the ball." This wasn't good. Not good at all. Venter's reputation among security circles as a fearless fighter was well earned. He wouldn't go down without a bloody fight, that much he knew. Engelbrecht dreaded to think what firepower was tucked into the guy's ankle holster and other places on his body. Same went for others. Unless they got them out of there pronto, he would be forced to pull out. A voice crackled in his ear. "What's it, Lieutenant?"

"SAPS Edendal circling beer tent, sir."

"Jesus, this is all we fokken need." An impending bloodbath was unfolding before his very eyes – accompanied by the image of a crazed pit bull released into a confined room of rats. Above him, in the far distance, he could hear the hovering chopper, awaiting his further instructions. He chewed on his cheek.

"Captain, SAPS Edendal now moving away from beer tent. Continuing due north." Engelbrecht heaved a sigh of relief. This was too close for comfort; he had to do something. "Sir!"

"What's it, Hans?"

"Ferreira and Botes heading away from south end. Both now going through Exit One."

Engelbrecht shut his eyes, grouping his thoughts. "Let me know when they start driving. Is Dippenaar out the pen yet?"

"Yes, sir. Him, plus white female and minor have climbed into black Navarra."

Potentially messy on the one hand. But on the other, it would work to Team Sky's advantage. "But still no fokken sign of Venter?"

"Nothing yet, Captain. SAPS Edendal still roaming the environs."

Engelbrecht had used up his nine lives. The time

had come to switch course, make some snap decisions. Dropping his chin, he barked into the mic. "Okay, manne, change of plan. Prepare to move in."

Emerging from the smoke and dust, the Neanderthal-like creature bore down on the huddle of terror awaiting the lethal blow that would deliver them into the hands of the ever-after.

But it never came.

"Out the way, mense!" shouted the policeman, leaping over the potjie pot, veering a sharp left and disappearing back into the smoke like some nightmarish apparition. Cantering close behind its master was a ginger-haired specimen with a red face, its gun drawn and at the ready.

Steve and Tarryn Aldridge slowly opened their eyes and looked around them, struggling to comprehend. An eerie silence had descended over the showgrounds. Alongside, the man in the Isuzu T-shirt and rugby shorts shrugged, then continued packing up his equipment.

Tarryn could barely manage a croaky whisper. "Steve?" Her husband stared back at her, even less capable of speech. "Are you thinking what I'm thinking?" She lifted her hand to her mouth, hoping against hope. Terror was fast giving way to bewildered relief. "Stevie?" Her husband nodded. "It wasn't us they were coming for."

Truter was running out of steam – the impressive leap over the potjie pot had been a leap too far. His knee was starting to protest in agony.

"Sir, are you okay?" puffed Delport at his shoulder.

"Of course I'm okay. Don't I look okay?" puffed Truter back. "You still have me covered, Delport?"

"Yes, sir!"

"Good!" Truter pulled up behind the ablution block. "We'll regroup here for a bit." He bent over, hands gripping his thighs, staring into the ground, trying to slow his spinning world.

"You sure you okay, sir?"

"All good, Delport, just dizzy." He looked up. People were staring. Waiting for his next move. "Put that bladdy gun away, Delport. You're making the mense nervous. And keep your voice down."

Delport quickly holstered his weapon. "Sorry. What about yours?"

Truter grunted, considered for a moment, then shoved his .38 into the back of his pants. "Can you see him?"

"Who, sir?"

"Jakkals Venter. What do you think we're doing here, man?"

"I didn't realise we were—"

Truter straightened up. "Don't worry, Delport. Like usual, you let me do all the heavy lifting. Wait here." Truter slid along the clinker brick wall and peered around the corner. "Waar die fok is jy?"

"Are you talking about the mayor, sir?" whispered Delport at his back. "Last time I heard him he was on the loudspeaker at the stage."

Truter stared up at the sky. "I know that! But did you not see him, moegoe?"

"No, sir. I didn't know that's who we were after. You didn't brief me—"

"Delport, you know what, you just keep me covered. And you keep quiet. I'll do the rest."

Sergeant Truter! Constable Delport! This is Captain Engelbrecht. Come in!

Delport reached towards his radio.

"Don't you bladdy answer that thing."

"But it's the second time he's—"

"As your commanding officer, Delport, I command you not to answer," hissed Truter. He was still peering around the wall, desperately scanning the area for Jakkals. He needed this more than anything. His future depended on it – his emotional, spiritual, and professional future depended on it. Above his head, a toilet flushed through the open window. Followed by the sound of a tap opening and whistling. His moment was slipping away from him. He clamped his eyes shut, unable to accept the unfolding reality. History was about to repeat itself all over. Just like last time, they were going to drag him across the burning coals, blame him for everything, then throw him to the dogs. This time there would be no coming back.

The guy inside the bogs was still whistling. From where or what he couldn't remember, but Truter knew the tune. Pressed against the wall, he fought back his tears –

tears of frustration and bitterness and twenty-five years of pain seeking relief. If anyone had deserved to bring Jakkals down, it was him, nobody else. He felt Delport at his back, waiting for his next move. He didn't dare turn and look him in the eyes; all Delport would see in his so-called superior was a FF – Fuck-up Failure. The hand drier inside the bogs had stopped running. He was still whistling. Somewhere between the pain and frustration and despair it came to him: "Forever Young" by that group Alphaville that they used to listen to all the time on the border—

Truter's skin had started to prickle. His pupils had started to dilate. His hands had turned clammy. His mouth had turned bone-dry. Behind him, as Delport would later recount in great detail, he watched, as if in slow motion, his commanding officer reach behind his back and in a Hollywood-choreographed sequence withdraw his .38, cock the hammer, arc it back round his body, and up to his chest. As he would also later recount in even greater detail, no sooner had Sergeant Truter demonstrated his amazing handling skills than Brits mayor and murderous life insurance syndicate ringleader Jakkals Dawid Venter stepped from the ablution block. Where subsequently, and to his total surprise and dismay, he encountered Sergeant Clinton Truter of SAPS Edendal ready and waiting to make the arrest of his professional career.

52

Sergeant Truter was content to let Delport do the talking. And just as well, because it would be several days before he understood the pieces of the puzzle. Besides, as he had iterated several times already to Constable Delport, he was a man of action, not empty words. Operation Red Jackal was proof in the pudding – if there was anything that South Africa needed right now, it was men of action.

Truter sat to one side nursing his knee with an icepack – he would have to pay Dr Santos a visit soon – observing Engelbrecht and the Special Task Team go about its mop-up operations. Behind him, Delport was cordoning off the area with yellow crime scene tape, struggling to keep the rubberneckers at bay. Jakkals Venter and Frederick Ferreira had been cuffed and read their rights and were now staring out forlornly from the behind the mesh of the black SCU (Special Canine Unit) Fortuner. For the past half-hour a rookie reporter from *North West Sun* (Cultural Events Supplement) had been going around interviewing witnesses, and was now angling for a one-on-one with Captain Johan Engelbrecht of the country's elite Special Crimes Unit. An SCU Falcon helicopter could be heard fast approaching from the west, carrying Conrad Botes and Juan Dippenaar. It would emerge that Botes had been intercepted and arrested on the N4 highway without so much as a single shot fired. As for Dippenaar, after a prolonged chase across the North West's backroads, the fugitive had abandoned his vehicle and wife, and fled into a nearby mielie field. After a brief exchange of fire, in which Dippenaar sustained a self-inflicted bullet wound to the foot, and a bite from a local farm dog, he was apprehended.

The reporter had now cornered Engelbrecht, with a circle of onlookers forming thick and fast around him. Engelbrecht beckoned over the sun-burnt heads.

"Please, mense, make an opening for our two police officers. They need to come through." Engelbrecht waited for Truter to limp across to the arena, assisted by a beaming and still red-faced Delport. "Welcome, boys." His stage set, Engelbrecht turned back to the reporter. "Ja, to get back to your question, it is thanks to the excellent detective work of these two police officers standing next to me, Sergeant Clinton Truter and Constable Delport, that we were able to make a number of critical arrests today in what has been an ongoing nationwide fraud investigation." He turned and spoke directly to the growing crowd. "The residents of Edendal can be proud to have men of such moral calibre and loyalty. Men who are willing to place the safety of their country over and above their own lives." Squeezing the PR moment – it was the least he could do for Truter – Engelbrecht turned to the two men, snapped to military attention, and saluted. "Sergeant Truter. Constable Delport. Your country thanks you!" On cue, a blast of spontaneous applause erupted from the crowd. This was way more than any of those present could have hoped for – a police drama included in the price of their Agri Fest entry ticket. Truter spotted his mom in the crowd and waved. Delport was still beaming. Engelbrecht turned back to the reporter. "Yes, we will be making further arrests in the days to come, but I'm unable to comment further at this point in time as the investigation is still *sub judice*. All I can say is, watch this space, people." Above them, the Falcon was coming in to land. And with yet another thrilling distraction on the cards, the crowd dispersed and hurried along to catch the action.

Engelbrecht turned back to the two officers. "Once again, nice one, boys. Who would have thought, hey?" He rolled his head from side to side in wonderment. "When I woke up this morning, this was *not* how I expected things to go." He reached out and shook Delport's hand. "Exemplary work, Constable. Absolutely top-drawer research and analysis."

"Thank you, sir!"

"But I must warn you … You had better get ready to pack your bags." Engelbrecht laughed. "Hey, don't look so worried, man. What I'm saying is Human Resources is going to be in touch with you very soon, because I reckon SCU could do with that brain of yours."

"Thank you, sir!"

Engelbrecht moved on to Truter. He smiled. A genuine smile. A human smile.

"Sergeant."

"Captain?"

"Good luck to you and your future career. You are a good man. And a good soldier."

Truter bit on his lip. "Thank you, Captain. I appreciate you saying that."

Engelbrecht saluted his comrade. Maybe it was just the late afternoon light, or maybe he was just imagining it. But there was a flame burning in Truter's eyes, a flame Engelbrecht had not noticed before.

53

Steve Aldridge caught himself giggling like a nervous schoolgirl as he worked the tow hitch. He couldn't work out why or what, but it was the best feeling in the world. For some reason it made him think of those Eastern Germans reuniting with their long-lost relatives in the West after the Berlin Wall fell. Same for the North Koreans who broke through the DMY, or whatever zone.

Aldridge pulled on the tow bar – nice and tight – and stood back and admired the result. Fortuner and Jurgens back together in perfect harmony, like it was meant to be from the very start.

For what had to now be the third time, he checked that the caravan door was locked – last thing they needed was for the door to swing open on the N3 and the Coleman to come flying out. Satisfied all was as it should be, he strolled to the front of the car. He had to hand it to Swanies; the mechanic had done a decent job with the new radiator. It was a thing of beauty, gleaming glossy black under the open bonnet, a symbol of long-lost freedom. Aldridge tapped the coolant reservoir and checked the radiator cap was screwed tight. He dropped the lid. All systems go.

Tarryn was waiting in the car, doing her make-up in the mirror. Her eyes shone under a layer of heavy mascara. "Can we go now?"

"Yep, I think we're all set." Aldridge turned the ignition. The Fortuner purred into life. He gave her a gentle rev. It was the nearest thing to a choir of angels.

"Well, then, let's get the flip out of this place, babes!"

Aldridge eased the Fortuner off the kerb. In the rear-view mirror, the Jurgens swayed gently from side to side. "Did you get to say bye?"

"Only to the wife. I still don't understand what she's doing with that prize A-hole."

"You shouldn't call …" Aldridge trailed off. For some reason he no longer cared.

"But I must say, she did seem much happier today."

"Wasn't she happy before?"

"No."

"I didn't notice."

"That's because you're a man. Girls have a sixth sense about these things. She had this glow to her face. Like she was in love or something."

"Definitely wouldn't be ... the prize A-hole."

Tarryn pushed back into the headrest and laughed. A proper laugh. "Geez, this isn't the Steve I know. Using foul language, and all. What's more, he's smiling!"

"I know. It feels like I'm floating in a dream. I can't actually believe we're driving out of this ... kakhole." To emphasise the point, Aldridge pressed his foot into the accelerator. To the front lay a new beginning. A new life.

"You're so right, it does feel like a dream. We've done well, babes. We've done so amazingly well. And do you notice something else?"

"What?"

"We're making small talk again."

"That is but true. We are."

"It feels nice. Like old times ... Hey, isn't that—"

"The guy who was staying at the B&B? It does look like him."

"It's definitely him, Steve. Poor man, he's not even carrying a suitcase, or anything. You think we should offer him a lift?"

"Do you think that's a good idea?"

"Why not, babes? He seems like a harmless sort."

"Ja, okay, but as long as we only take him as far as the Engen on the N3. He'll easily get another lift from there." Aldridge slowed the Fortuner and pulled off the road. He kept watch in the side mirror. "I don't think he's clicked that we've stopped for him. He's still just standing there."

"Maybe you should hoot?"

"Good idea … Okay, he's coming now. You're right, he has nothing with him. Nothing but the clothes on his back."

"I wonder where he's going to?"

"We'll ask him … He's coming round to your side." Aldridge dropped Tarryn's window.

"Evenings!" said the hitchhiker. A gap-toothed grin was plastered across his face.

"Hi there," said Tarryn. "Where are you going to?"

"Joburg, ma'am. To the big city lights."

Aldridge leant across. "We're going north, but if you want, we can take you to the One-Stop on the N3. Will that be okay?"

"Will that be okay? My friend, that will be perfecto!"

Without further prompting, the back door opened and the man squeezed in behind Tarryn.

"You can move that trophy across. Do you have enough leg space? I can move my seat forwards."

"No worries, ma'am, I'm snug as a bug in a rug. And I'm very grateful to you good people. Catching a lift isn't so easy these days. Because why? Nobody trusts nobody any more. That's what I call tragic!"

"That is true. But we recognised you from the guesthouse. We were also staying there."

"Is that now right? Well, nice to meet some genuine people finally."

"By the way, I'm Steve, and this is my wife, Tarryn."

"Honoured to meet you, Steve and Tarryn. You've done well for yourself, sir. Lovely car. Lovely caravan. Lovely wife."

Aldridge gave Tarryn's knee a squeeze, looked up in the rear-view and winked. "Thanks, I know. I've done very well for myself."

Tarryn turned in her seat. "What's your name?"

"My name?"

"Yes."

Cliffie Abrahams smiled. A confident self-knowing smile. He gazed out the window at the distant orange glow descending over Mother Africa. He patted the thick envelope in his jacket pocket. "The name is Johnson. Gary Johnson."

Epilogue

Kruger Tourist Stumbles on Gruesome Scene

Correspondent – A British tourist yesterday came across a gruesome scene in the Kruger National Park. According to Park spokeswoman Lettie Nieuwoudt, the unnamed tourist and his family were staying at Olifants Camp. They were on an early morning game drive in their hired car when they came across what initially appeared to them to be an animal kill at the side of the road. On closer inspection they discovered to their horror a dismembered human head. They immediately reported the find to the Kruger authorities, who cordoned off the area to the public. The police arrived several hours later, by which time the head had allegedly been dragged off into the bush by an animal – most likely a hyena, according to Nieuwoudt. Trackers are still searching for it. Authorities believe the head belonged to a person attempting to enter South Africa illegally from Mozambique, and was killed during the night by lions. According to Nieuwoudt, lion attacks on illegal migrants are believed to be relatively common. In most cases, however, there would be very little evidence by way of human remains. The police are investigating further.

Enjoyed this book?

Feel free to post your review at www.redpress.co.za

Interested in more by Paul Leger?

Visit www.paulleger.co.za

The author

Born and bred in the Free State gold mining town of Virginia, Paul Leger stumbled through a degree in Journalism and Psychology at Rhodes University, followed by a brief stint as an academic researcher. Fleeing the ivory tower, he's since made intermittent stabs at a writing career, laying claim to SA's first guide to mountain biking, six editions of the popular *Guide to Budget Getaways*, and the autobiographical novel, *Sean, Eddie and Me*. *Roadkill* is his second novel.